Praise for V

'A carefully crafted littl[...]
—THE ADVERTISER

'Lohrey achieves a kind of perfection ...'
—THE SYDNEY MORNING HERALD

'Extraordinarily vivid and compelling ...
A stunning and memorable novella.'
—THE AGE

'This finely crafted novella took my breath away.'
—THE MERCURY MAGAZINE

'Vertigo *will keep you up much too late
but it's worth a one-sitting read.*'
—THE WEST AUSTRALIAN

'There is something enormously satisfying, both
aesthetically and morally, about this delicate
tale, as sense that – as with a perfectly executed
piece of music – no mistakes have been made.'
—AUSTRALIAN BOOK REVIEW

Vertigo

Published by Black Inc.,
an imprint of Schwartz Books Pty Ltd
Wurundjeri Country
22–24 Northumberland Street
Collingwood VIC 3066, Australia
enquiries@blackincbooks.com
www.blackincbooks.com

9781863954303 (paperback)
9781921870026 (ebook)

 A catalogue record for this
book is available from the
National Library of Australia

Book design by Thomas Deverall
Images © Lorraine Biggs 2009

Printed in Australia by McPherson's Printing Group.

VERTIGO

a pastoral

Amanda Lohrey

with images by Lorraine Biggs

Black Inc.

I

LUKE WORLEY GREW UP ON the edge of the city, in a neat suburban garden with a green lawn and a date palm, and in all that time he never developed the least interest in birds, not even, as a boy, to throw stones at. But now, at the age of thirty-four, he has taken to bird-watching. It's true he might once have laughed at this, but since then much has changed. Now, with his wife Anna, he has moved to the coast.

There are birds in the city, but in the city you rarely notice them; there is too much urban jazz in the air: the drone of jets roaring in, the manic whine of sirens or the thumping bass line of a neighbour's latest dance-music craze. Near Luke's apartment block there was a mournful bird cry that could be heard at around three in the morning when he happened to wake in the dark, perhaps from a bad dream, but somehow he never got around to identifying it. He meant to, but it was one of those things that fell out of your head with the hot monsoonal wash of an early morning shower or your first avid gulp of coffee. On one occasion he did think to ask friends who lived in the same street if they knew the bird with the mournful call, and while they, too, had heard the sound, and could imitate it over a drink, no-one could say what it looked like. He thought his parents might know – older people knew things like that – but Ken and Marg proved to be as ignorant as anyone. Ken was unable, when pressed over dinner, to distinguish with certainty between a raven and a blackbird. So much for the wisdom of the elders.

When interest rates rose for the third time in eighteen months, he and Anna despaired of ever buying in the city. In the first weeks of winter, Anna developed a chest infection she couldn't shake and when diagnosed with asthma, she took it badly; it made her feel like an invalid. It was Anna who prided herself on her fitness; it was she who went jogging every morning around Sydney University oval (Luke was the couch potato, always with his nose in a book) and now she was being told that for a long time, perhaps even decades, she would have to inhale steroids. For days she felt weepy and vulnerable, as if she were no longer the person she thought she was, or had willed herself to be. As for Luke, for the first time ever he felt his innate optimism beginning to metabolise into something jittery. That burnish of rough glamour that had once overlaid his city seemed suddenly shabby. He could feel the future coming towards him, indeed it was almost at his door, and it was not what he had hoped for.

In the past he had felt free of encumbrance, had looked on as his friends locked themselves into immense mortgages from which they saw no escape. Now, absurdly, he began to feel burdened by his inability to shoulder the very debt that he had once scorned. Was this a muddle? Yes, it was. The clarity of thought that enlightened his twenties had begun to darken, in the way that a smog haze settles by degrees over a bright morning.

The moment of truth arrived late one night as he lay in bed with his wife. Outside the rain was hurtling down; inside they were breathing mould and damp. Anna was propped up awkwardly with pillows, wheezing and sucking in gasps of Ventolin from the small metal tube of her inhaler. Her short blond hair stuck to her skin in limp strands and when she slumped back against the wall, sallow and greyish, he knew it was time to go. He could not bear to see her deflated and diminished in this way. It was as if her robust beauty, an athletic glow that had first attracted him, was being preyed upon by an invisible vampire.

The next evening, over dinner, he broached his proposal, and found her receptive.

'Wouldn't you miss the city?'

'I might. I wouldn't know until I tried it.'

And so, in a moment, the ground shifted. They would move to the country and work from home; they would look for an affordable house and if they couldn't find one they would rent. As editors of corporate and legal documents they could transfer their small business to just about anywhere; they were established, and in the past twelve months had scarcely been able to keep up with demand.

'We'll give it two years,' Luke told his bemused parents. 'It's not as if it's a life sentence.'

'I warned you about living in Bridge Road,' his father said. 'It's all that fine particle pollution, it dehydrates the organs. In parts of Los Angeles, babies are being born with shrunken hearts.'

Good old Ken; always the optimist.

Anna's GP cautioned them against the country. 'Asthma rates are just as high in rural areas,' she said, 'if not more so. It's the wheat dust, among other things.'

'Well, then,' said Luke, 'we won't settle in wheat country.'

To her friends, Anna appeared to put up little resistance to this migration and they assumed she was concerned about her health. What they couldn't know, because she didn't tell them, was that like her husband she found herself troubled by a falling away of her youthful élan. There was so much money around, a dizzying spiral of excess, and yet she and Luke struggled. They worked long hours but still they could not afford anything better than the rental on their cramped apartment. The paint on the ceilings was cracked and peeling and the rooms were dark with a sombre brown varnish on the woodwork. At dinner parties people spoke solemnly of their renovations; with the air of diplomats renegotiating the Geneva Convention they discoursed on the problem of installing a second bathroom, or whether they could trust advice from their broker on how to finesse their share portfolio in a volatile market.

When she was in her twenties Anna had thought of herself as bohemian, a free spirit who was serious about the right things and carefree about the rest, but now she was turning into some other woman, a woman on the edge of becoming anxiously acquisitive. Though scornful of the crass material ambitions of others, she was secretly ashamed of the shabbiness of her apartment, and fed up with cheap holidays. But this was only material lack; what was worse was the corrosive effect on her goodwill towards the world. That most acidic of beasts, envy, had a fang-hold on her heart. She was past thirty, she was in a spiritual impasse and she needed to find a way out of it.

One quiet Sunday afternoon they opened the glove box of their car, took out an assortment of road maps and laid them out across the kitchen table. Their first task was to get oriented, to compile a list of rural towns and coastal hamlets that had good mobile access and reliable broadband.

Next they Googled these on tourist websites to
see if they liked the lie of the land; they knew
these virtual postcards could be deceptive but
still, it was a beginning, and when they had agreed
on a short-list they set off on weekend reconnaissance. Once out on the open road they felt free
again: the further away from the city they drove,
the more the world expanded into a mysterious
limbo, a potential space waiting to be filled. And
to their great delight, on each of these journeys
the boy chose to accompany them. In the claustrophobic spaces of their dark little apartment
his appearances were erratic and unpredictable,
but once out on the freeway they would glance
behind them and there he would be, lap-sashed
on the back seat and with an inquiring look on his
face; that dreamy, expectant expression that children get when they are travelling to an unknown
destination.

And how little they knew about 'out there'.
Some inland towns stood frozen in time: a dusty
high street; a melancholy war memorial; perhaps
a faded Mechanics Institute from the 1920s; a café

with chipped laminex tables; a general store with window displays of headless wooden dummies in drab clothing. But there were other towns that could almost have been outposts of the city, where an art gallery with kelim rugs and carved wooden birds might be found beside a sleek new wine bar. The Worleys agreed that they wanted to live in neither, not the old or the new, although what exactly they were looking for they couldn't say. Then, late one Saturday afternoon, in a fit of irritable fatigue, they took a wrong turn-off and drove into the small coastal hamlet of Garra Nalla.

Garra Nalla could scarcely be described as a town. It was a settlement of eighty or so houses, each one nestled in among a grey-green cluster of casuarinas and shaggy old banksias laden with masses of black seed cobs. The turn-off led straight to a wild beach and as they caught their first glimpse of breaking surf the boy suddenly sat upright. Roused from his torpor on the back seat he craned his neck to see out, and wriggling free of his seatbelt scrambled up onto the seat to press his face against the window.

The road in ran alongside a narrow brown river that flowed into the sea through a sandy trench. Beyond the river lay a wide lagoon, sheltered behind a ridge of sandhills and on the other side of the sandhills was a long white beach. On the near side of the river lay the hamlet of Garra Nalla. The approach to the settlement was an avenue of flowering gums, a palette of pinks and orange and gold, and yes they were pretty, but almost too picturesque, thought Anna, like a crudely printed postcard. It was the she-oaks that engaged her, soft clusters of them dotted among the houses; a subtle blur of fine filaments swaying against the sky, or drooping to the ground in wispy canopies.

Slowly they drove down the dusty unsealed roads and could see that most of the shacks in the settlement were fibro or timber, and shielded from the rocky foreshore by dense thickets of tea-tree and boobialla. There were no letter-boxes and no street lights. They drove up to the grassy windswept headland and looked out to a wild arc of the coastline, framed at its northern end by a rocky outcrop known as Rittler's Point and at its southern end by the settlement of Garra Nalla. Here, where they stood, it was bare save for three great Norfolk pines that must surely have been planted in the colonial era and that loomed above them now like sentinels. They could see where the ocean tides flowed into the river, and how at high tide the shallow trench would rise in depth until it merged with the lagoon. But on this day the tide was out and the lagoon so uneven that it emerged in a pattern of curved sandbanks and warm, shallow pools. It was only in its north-western corner, furthest from the ocean, that the broadwater remained both deep and still, and here it was graced by a colony of black swans.

For a long time the three of them stood at the edge of the headland, gazing out to sea. The incoming waves swept into a narrow canyon beneath their feet where, after a momentary stillness, a curtain of white water reared into the air, drenching them in spray. As each wave came crashing into the blowhole the boy hunched his shoulders in anticipation and as the cloud of salty spume sprayed above them he shrieked with delight, his feet running up and down on the spot with excitement. And they laughed, and wondered how on earth a place of such grandeur had escaped development. Why wasn't it a resort?

By the time they started home it was late and they stopped for a meal at the nearby town of Brockwood, and fell into conversation with the waiter who warned them that the beach at Garra Nalla was known for its dangerous rip. Four people had drowned there in the past five years. Only a fool would swim there and tourists gave it a wide berth.

Perfect, they thought; *just perfect*.

'But there's nothing here!' their friends would exclaim when later they came to visit. No shops, no hotel, no community hall, no boat ramp or barbecue area. And this was true, and it was the reason they had chosen the place. They felt that in some essential way it was uncultivated, a landscape out of time, and as such it could not define them. Here they could live, and simply be.

And then there was the house, a weatherboard homestead from the Federation era with a gabled roof and dilapidated gravitas they yearned to restore. It had a stately hallway down the middle and a wide veranda on three sides, and while it did not directly overlook the water, the beach was only an eight-minute walk away. There was a big farm kitchen of spacious intimacy and all of the rooms were square, so that no matter where you stood in the house the proportions seemed somehow right, with you at the centre. In every room there was a fireplace, and at the heart of the kitchen was an old cast-iron stove with black enamelled doors and a tin flue that disappeared into the ceiling. When the agent remarked to the Worleys on how easily the stove could be removed, they looked at one another with the same thought: they would keep it. It came with a boiler that heated the hot water and they would learn how to fire the slow combustion oven. Here, at last, they would have their own elemental hearth. As for the asking price on the property, they could scarcely believe their luck; because it had no water views the house had been classified as just another run-down rural homestead. With the help of Luke's parents and Anna's mother, they financed the loan.

There were nights when Anna lay in bed with last-minute misgivings but Luke, typically, was resolute. And so, in the middle of a humid January, they packed up and moved, though not before Luke had upgraded their espresso machine to a more expensive model. When friends joked about the perils of rural living, of snakes, bushfire and drought, he assumed a deadpan expression. 'Not a problem,' he said. 'It's the coffee I'm worried about.'

...

Their first night.

It was just after seven on a mellow Saturday evening when they turned off the highway and drove into Garra Nalla. A deep coral sunset flared along the ridge of the western hills; beside the silent headland the lagoon glittered in a wash of silvery pink. The house was musty and dark but when they entered its cobwebbed hall they trembled with a frisson that could only be described as ownership; it was as if the house had been waiting for them. While they unpacked, the boy prowled through the house on his own so that they could hear the squeak of doors along the hallway and the creak of floorboards as he peered into the corners of empty rooms. He was way ahead of them, and he was restless.

That night, on a mattress on the floor, they lay in one another's arms and looked up through the unclad window to a moon swollen with radiance. Anna was too excited to sleep; for a time she would drift off, and then wake in a state of relaxed alertness. On the roof a family of possums hissed and snarled like devils, riffs of such comic malevolence that they only made her smile, but the boy was afraid and would not settle. For a long time he wandered up and down the hallway, until at last she called to him through the gloom and he came and nestled beside her at the edge of the mattress. But still he was agitated, and his tiny limbs jerked, so that she pulled the white sheet up to his chin and kissed his blond curls, and stroked the delicate hollow between his shoulder-blades until he was becalmed in sleep.

*

Now instead of heading for a coffee-shop on Saturday mornings they lounge together on the wide veranda. Luke, the early riser, has taken his breakfast outside and as Anna opens the screen door to join him, she looks around absentmind-edly for the boy. It's almost as if she expects him to be here every morning, and she must be careful of this; if she begins to take anything for granted, anything at all, then she might break the spell.

Lazily they begin to browse through the thick

weekend papers that Luke has collected from a shop ten kilometres down the highway, but before long these have been left to lie scattered on the deck while they sit quietly outside the kitchen window, staring intently at two small birds that feed in one of the river wattles near the back door. Luke has fetched his binoculars, but he is having trouble adjusting the focus. The binoculars are new, a present from Anna.

'Take your glasses off,' she says. God, he's so impractical. Clever, but always slightly distracted and sometimes, even, clumsy. It worries her that in the country, where men are expected to do much of their own maintenance and repairs, he will not be able to keep up with the demands of their run-down property.

Luke continues to fiddle with the focus. 'Get the bird book out,' he whispers. 'It's on the coffee-table in the living room. Quick, before they fly away.'

Anna returns with their newly purchased copy of Simpson and Day's *Field Guide to the Birds of Australia*.

'Just get a pad,' says Luke, 'and write down the markings. We can look it up later.'

She perches on the edge of the cane extender. 'Okay, fire away.'

'Well, it's got that pale green chest, obviously, and a yellowish head with little white stripes across the top. And it's got black stripes along the edges of its wings.'

'What colour is the beak?'

'The beak is … is … dark grey, I think, I can't quite see … damn, it's flown off. I'll try and spot the other one.' He turns his head to the left and scans the fine lacy foliage of the wattle. 'Nope, can't find it. They've both gone.' He puts down the binoculars. 'Show me the book. I'll identify it while it's fresh in my mind.'

Of course, he can't. It's only in the evening when they are sitting on the veranda after dinner that Anna finds the colour plate that she is sure closely resembles what she observed with her naked eye. 'Look,' she says, 'that's it. Striated Pardalote. It says here they're migratory birds who travel south in spring to breed and fly away in winter. They can be identified by their yellow eyebrow and white striations on the crown. Striations,' she adds emphatically, 'not spots.'

'Show me.' He takes the book from her and stares at the colour plate. 'Brilliant,' he says. And they go to bed with a sense of satisfaction. They've only been on the coast a month and already they have identified a pardalote. Until now they had never even heard of one.

This house. This house is their kingdom. It's as if they were dispossessed of this house at birth and have at last reclaimed their entitlement. Instead of being confined to a boxed-in apartment they are free now to roam through its many rooms, to experience the joy of nooks and alcoves, not to mention their favourite hang-out, the wide veranda. In the city they had a small balcony off their apartment, but it wasn't the same. You looked out to a smoggy curtain across the built-up sky or down a long drop to the bitumen road below. You were not earthed. What you desired was a space between two worlds, that dream-like threshold where you are neither in nor out but floating in a cradle of space, but you wanted also at any moment to be able to step off the veranda and onto firm ground. You were an earth animal, not a bird; you did not want to nest in the sky.

And the boy, too, loves the veranda; he likes to run the full length of it, trailing a long stick behind him that makes a loud, rackety clattering sound. Along the south corner Luke has strung up a rainbow-striped hammock and sometimes they look out on a still day and see the hammock swinging wildly and they know that the boy is enveloped in its folds.

In the city Luke rented a one-room office in a renovated warehouse while Anna worked from home in a tiny second bedroom overlooking a grimy fire-escape. Here, Luke has only to climb a let-down ladder to his sun-struck eyrie in the roof, a glassed-in attic he has converted into an office, while Anna retires to the back sunroom where she can look west to the smoky blue hills. He rises early, she tends to sleep in, but on all other fronts they observe a strict discipline. They even take their coffee breaks separately because it would be too easy to lounge together in the shade of the veranda and drift for an hour into idle conversation. Often Luke will carry his coffee out to the rickety Juliet balcony off the attic, for it looks across to the ocean and here he can study the local surfers, those sleek wetsuited truants of the moment. He thinks of them as black birds of the surf, paddling out beyond the reef off Rittler's Point and riding the autumn swells in lithe, crouching postures so that they resemble some weird form of sea-bird looking for a kill.

Early in March they prepare a garden. They work in the late afternoons, digging into a sandy soil flecked with greyish white fragments of shell that tell them they are working over a midden. Luke uses some old fence palings to box in two vegetable beds and buys a trailer-load of rich brown soil from a farmer in the hills. He covers it all with green shade-cloth stretched over a structure of rubber tubing because the sun is too hot and without shade the seedlings will burn. Before they came to Garra Nalla, neither of them had used so much as a trowel. Now they have calluses on their hands and the pleasure of rhythmic physical movements, like raking leaves, can bring on a state of mindless contentment. Often the boy appears to play alongside them, whirling around in the dust or darting mischievously among the weed piles and throwing clumps of weed into the air. Sometimes he sings snatches of nursery songs in a thin, childish lilt that is charmingly off-key. At such times his parents do not look one another in the eye; the weighty joy of it would be too much.

But this is not Eden, this is drought country. Behind the coast are hills of dry sclerophyll forest and between the hamlet and the forest are pastures cleared for sheep, grasslands that are dried out and dun-coloured from seven years of drought. There is rain in the hills, though not as much as there used to be, and there are times when the locals gaze up longingly at the caressing mist that occasionally settles over the low peaks on the horizon. Seven years of drought: it has begun to sound biblical; a curse.

When first they moved in, the water level in their tanks was alarmingly low and now they set buckets beneath the shower for the first run-off, wash the vegetables in a mixing bowl, drain the water into a second bucket and strain the remains of the teapot into a big ice-cream container. When they renovate, they will replace the lavatory cisterns, but this is complicated, for the new minimal-flush patent is a problem with septic tanks and blockages are frequent.

There are days when they speak only of water.

Their nearest neighbour is an elderly widower, Gilbert Reilly, who made himself known to them soon after they moved in. Gil is tall with a long beaky nose and ginger-grey hair that is thin on top. He has taken to dropping by for a coffee and what he calls a 'natter' and mostly they encourage this because Gil is a mine of local folklore. Not only that, he is happy to advise them on how to work the wood stove: the kind of dry wood they need and where to get it; how to avoid a build-up of creosote; how to bank and dampen the fire. And Gil approves of the new settlers, the sea changers. 'They bring a bit of life to the district,' he says, 'and you can't expect things to stay the same.' He himself has four grown-up children who live elsewhere. They rarely return to visit their father, but Gil claims not to hold this against them. 'Too expensive for 'em to travel often,' he says. 'Mortgages are tough now.' This is one of the reasons they like him: he is not one of those old codgers who drone on about the good old days.

On the other side of them is Rodney Banfield, the local plumber, a short, thickset man in his late twenties with a long blond pony-tail and an ugly dog, a black Staffordshire cross that barks and barks and barks all night until Rodney comes home in the small hours of the morning. His shack is a fibro box painted a deep pink with a large satellite dish on the roof and a small deck featuring an array of decrepit vinyl armchairs. But Rodney is not always there. He waits for his girlfriend's husband to fly inland to the mine for his two-week shift so that Rodney can moonlight in the miner's bed with the miner's wife. This is not a happy situation and the smell of trouble drifts in the air on those nights when Rodney is banished back to base camp to sit out on his boxy deck, to brood and smoke. At the bottom of his block he keeps a shed where often the light is on overnight and Luke suspects an indoor dope garden, which is nothing compared to the plantation Rodney is rumoured to be growing in the hills.

In April the weather begins to cool and Luke buys a wetsuit, but soon realises that he prefers walking to swimming and if he goes to the beach in two

minds, in his wetsuit, then once he has swum the
lagoon he can't walk in the suit without chafing.
After a while he tires of the effort to struggle into
and out of this latex corset and the wetsuit hangs
in the wardrobe like a ghostly frogman. He is less
an active participant in Nature, he jokes to Anna,
than an observer, and he marvels at how easy it is
on his walks to become mesmerised by the bird-
life: black cormorants perched beside the lagoon,
lusty pelicans lolling on sandbanks at low tide,
opportunistic Pacific gulls cruising the shoreline.
Sometimes he sees a pair of red-eyed sooty oystercatchers, and out to sea the big white gannets with
sword-like beaks, diving at sudden and electrify-
ing speeds into schools of mackerel that tremor
below the surface. Best of all are the black swans
that congregate in the north-west corner of the
lagoon. Only once has he come upon a swan swimming in close, but as he approached it began to
paddle furiously across the surface of the water,
rearing up suddenly to reveal a flash of white tail
feather before soaring into the sky like a phallic
arrowhead.

One late afternoon around dusk, returning home from a walk along the rocks, he opens the side gate beside a shaggy old banksia tree and there on a low bough, at eye level, is a bird he does not recognise. It looks like an owl. Normally the birds in the garden are skittish and fly away when he approaches, but this one gazes back at him with the utmost composure so that he feels he could reach out and stroke its grey speckled feathers. Instead he just stares into its eyes, and the weird thing is this: the bird stares back. It looks right at him, and in that moment of looking a current passes between them, a soundless exchange of energy. He feels his breathing slow, and the strange, almost painful sensation of his heart expanding in the cavity of his chest. There is no time: time is a loop of endless return, a return to this moment, which is not strange but a coming home, and it does not occur to him to ask where this home is because he is simply there, he is in it; this silent space of euphoric emptiness. And for the rest of his walk home he is elated. He has never been happier; pointlessly, mindlessly happy.

That night he scans the book for an image of the bird on the bough but is unable to find anything that remotely resembles it. At first this bothers him (he likes to put a name to things), but after an hour of fruitless searching he lays the book aside. Seeing the bird, he tells Anna, is more important than the naming of it. It's like the boy, he reflects; they've never named the boy, and it doesn't matter, indeed it's better that way. Lying in the dark, just before sleep, he thinks of how much he would have liked it if the boy had been there with him, if he too had been able to see the bird, and be seen by it. But he has no control over the boy, who comes and goes as he pleases.

And yet, the next morning when he goes out to chop wood for the stove, who should be there but the boy, poking at the woodpile with a long stick in the hope that the blue-tongue lizard that lurks in the crevices will dart out into the open. Sometimes the boy can look like an angel, polished by the sun, but today he is a bush urchin; on his left shin is a large purple bruise and his hair is matted with dirt. Seeing Luke approach, he whoops loudly and bangs his stick on the wood block as if performing a karate chop before running off to scatter a small party of New Holland honeyeaters that has alighted on a feed-tray of over-ripe figs, laid out for them on the grass by Anna. In an instant the boy has disappeared behind the far corner of the house where the river wattles grow and the honeyeaters, brash and undeterred, return to forage for their breakfast.

Often in the mild evenings after dinner Luke will go for a walk, straying far along the highway that runs beside the coast. On the other side of the highway from Garra Nalla and set among the yellow grasslands is an old squatter's mansion, built of stone. From the road, only the fanlights of its Georgian windows are visible and the vaulting of its enormous roof; the rest is obscured by a built-up mound of earth topped with stone ramparts. Along the sides and to the rear there are stone barns and stables, and here and there an old stone cottage with a derelict shingle roof, so that the whole settlement has the air of an abandoned compound, handsome but sinister.

One evening he takes Anna with him to show her the house and they climb the barbed-wire fence and approach the compound. Soon they are close enough to the built-up mound to see that along its stone ramparts there are narrow rectangular slits for firearms, and they realise they are looking at some kind of colonial fortification.

Later they ask Gil about the big house and he tells them it was bought up two years ago by a consortium of businessmen. The new owners have no interest in mixing with the locals; they fly in their city friends for weekend parties and it is clear that Gil does not warm to them; he preferred the old squatter's family, the McKinnons, for whom he had worked as a shearer and a roustabout. They knew how to get along with everyone. From time to time they turned up at community events and when they did, they knew people's names. They loaned equipment for emergency situations and their sons did their bit in the volunteer fire service. But not long after the

old man died, the elder son, Dugald, went swimming off the wild beach around Rittler's Point,
got caught in a rip and drowned. The property,
which had been in the family for almost a cen-
tury, was sold to the consortium.

And the fortifications?

'Bushrangers,' says Gil. 'And the blacks, of
course. Every now and then they'd make a raid on
the sheep, or worse.' Gil also tells them that the
area along the coast was once known as Ross's
Farm but that when the land behind the headland
was sold off for houses in the nineteen-twenties
they gave it the name of Garra Nalla, which was
the name the local tribespeople had for it.

'Who was Ross?'

'Some old soldier-settler who shot himself.
Tried to farm along the coastal strip after the first
War and had a bad go of it.'

'Someone is always trying to shoot something
around here,' Gil had said when they asked him
about the history of the settlement and he described how, late last autumn, he had heard gun-

shots coming from the marshlands at the edge of the lagoon. When he strolled over to investigate, he came upon the consortium's overseer and some of the weekenders shooting at the swans. Confronted by Gil, they claimed to have a permit, because the swans were eating the turnips sowed for stock feed, but Gil rang the police and demanded they come and put a stop to it. The shooting was a danger to anyone walking in the sandhills, he said, and because the local constable was a nephew of Gil's he drove in and called a halt.

Later, Gil confided that his mother used to 'bake the occasional swan.' They were good eating, he said, like goose; oily and gamey. 'Us kids used to collect the eggs over in the corner of the lagoon where they had their nests. Big things, like this.' He cupped his swollen and arthritic hands. 'Made the best scrambled eggs.'

In the fourth month of their migration, Anna sees a scrawled FOR SALE notice in the window of the supermarket in Brockwood. While Luke is on one of his bird-watching walks, she drives over to the neighbouring settlement behind Rittler's Point and buys a weathered yellow canoe, a surprise birthday present. The owner, a young surfie called Jacob, agrees to come over one weekend and give them some pointers on how to handle the canoe. Neither she nor Luke has ever paddled anything in their lives before, but with an afternoon's coaching from Jacob, a lithe, sunburnt boy, they begin to get the hang of it. Afterwards they invite Jacob back to the house for a beer but he declines. 'Have to pick up a mate,' he mumbles and then, as he climbs into his father's white Toyota ute: 'Watch out for the swans,' he says. 'If you get too close, they'll go you.' He grins. 'They think they own the place.'

Soon, in the late afternoons, they are gliding across the still black water, paddling stroke by slow stroke into a hot dusk. From across the lagoon they can hear the sounds of children careening around the headland on their bikes, their shouts echoing out over the water. Lights come on in the houses and the flares of home-coming high-beams light up the distant ribbon of road. On some evenings the boy comes with them, sitting deep in the canoe on the floor between their knees. He seems to like being on the water, except when the swans are near. Then his little body becomes stiff and hyper-alert, and he looks up anxiously to scan the sky.

It's around this time that Luke has the first in a series of recurring dreams. He dreams of a tidal wave that sweeps in from the ocean and submerges the settlement in a depth of clear green water. But this isn't a nightmare; it's a benign dream, a dream in which he swims beneath the sunlit surface like a water baby. And the boy is there, swimming alongside. His face is radiant and there are small translucent fish darting around his head; his golden curls stream behind him in unravelling coils of light while his small but supple limbs beat against the current.

*

The nights in Garra Nalla are quiet and it's then that Luke likes to read. All day he works onscreen and at night he has no desire to engage with it further, least of all to blog. He leaves it to Anna to catch up with friends, to post news of their sea change and to write those jokey accounts of rural mishaps that bear no true resemblance to the mysterious charm of their life here. Often he reads in bed while Anna, the night-owl, trawls through the cable news networks with their blaring live footage that can sometimes get on his nerves. It's a habit she got into as a teenager, before her father died. Her father, who worked long hours, was a news junkie, and if she wanted his company she had to sit up with him on the couch, watching the late news and documentaries. While he ate and drank the supper she prepared for him, he would comment on the events happening onscreen and it was then she felt close to him, like an adult he had taken into his confidence. Now, here in Garra Nalla, she has BBC and CNN: they make her feel connected to the outside world.

Behind the house is an old shed, like an outdoor dunny, and not long after they arrived Luke broke the padlock to discover two trunks crammed with antique hardbacks. 'The Dead Sea Scrolls', he jokingly dubbed them, for when he opened the larger of the two trunks the dust rose into his nostrils until he was convulsed by a sneezing fit and had to back out into the fresh air before returning to drag the trunks onto the grass. Each trunk bore a brass plate engraved with the name *A.E. Henley Esq.* and he guessed that they must be the property of a previous owner. He enquired at the Brockwood library and found that yes, the Reverend Henley had retired to Garra Nalla in the late sixties after two decades as the Anglican vicar of Brockwood. When the Reverend died, his house was auctioned off with all goods and chattels, including a large library of books, but the trunks must have been overlooked and left to moulder in the shed.

The odd thing about the vicar's collection is this: there is precious little theology in it and a great deal of travel writing, strange works like *Travels in Mesopotamia* by Col. George Hedley-Smythe, *A Thousand Miles up the Nile* by Miss Amelia B. Edwards and *The English in the West Indies* by J.A. Froude. With their marbled endpapers and silk ribbon markers, their gothic plates in black and white – 'the author's own engravings' – these exotic tomes are unlike anything Luke has read in the past.

Tonight he is about to give himself over to one of these volumes, *The Land That Is Desolate.* It's an imposing object, solid and stiff with a cover of coarse red linen and a title embossed in gold lettering, and it appears that the author was a notable in his day, an eminent physician, Sir Frederick Treves, Bart, G.C.V.O., C.B., LL.D., surgeon to His Majesty King Edward VII.

The Land That Is Desolate, subtitled 'An Account of a Tour in Palestine', is a travel diary, published in 1913. When first he delved into the vicar's collection, Luke had been intrigued to find a book that pre-dated the creation of Israel and the PLO, one in which Sir Frederick's own crude black and white photographs suggested nothing so much as a frozen stillness, the very antithesis of what now appears on the nightly news. Luke had forgotten about this book until, watching the news last night and the latest footage of a rocket strike in Gaza, it popped into his head; he would welcome some insight into the history of Palestine and he went out to the shed to dust off Sir Frederick and bring him inside.

But Treves is not at all what he expected, not some sanctimonious Edwardian pilgrim but a man of science with a cold eye for fakery. In mourning for the death of his daughter he has embarked on a journey to the source of all meaning, but from the moment he arrives in the Holy Land, Sir Frederick is acerbic and disgruntled. At every stop along the way, every crumbling town or dusty village, he is pestered by touts making extravagant claims for holy relics, and within the sacred spaces of the great churches he is roused by a Protestant dislike of priests and gaudy altars. Even Nature itself disappoints him, and his description of the biblical landscape is unremittingly bleak. '*The Promised Land has been for centuries ravaged by war and torn by internal dissension. It has been plundered and laid waste. Its inhabitants have been blotted out, its forests have been recklessly cut down and woods rooted up. The rainfall has in consequence diminished so that the land has dried up. Vineyard terraces have fallen into ruin and water channels into decay. Obsolete processes of cultivation have been maintained, the people have been harassed and oppressed until there is little joy in them. All this might have been foreshadowed in the deeds of the Book of the Chronicles of the Kings of Israel: "Ye shall ... fell every good tree, and mar every good piece of land with stones."*'

As Luke reads on, it becomes clear that no corner of this sacred terrain will be spared Sir

Frederick's unflinching appraisal. The desert of Judea is a *'mean country'*; the River Jordan a *'muddy stream'*; the town of Bethlehem is *'un-redeemably ugly'* and the road to Bethlehem *'traverses a poor, bare, and colourless country, unfriendly and unlovable, where the land is tree-less but for a few mendicant olives.'*

A few mendicant olives? It reminds Luke of the new olive plantation along the coast that belongs to a man called Haremza, an ex-surfing champion who has bought up a stretch of Ross's original farm and planted four thousand olive trees. A sign of the times, he thinks; olives, vine-yards, walnut farms. The old-style selectors are gone and change is everywhere, and now he and Anna are a part of it. And with this encourag-ing thought he puts down his book and walks to the window where the blinds remain furled and big cigar moths beat against the glass. Only the stars at night seem fixed in their station, and this, too, he knows is an illusion. Still, there are nights like this one when often he closes his book and wanders out to the edge of the veranda to gaze up in awe at the perfection of the dark, at stars so numerous that a profligate god might have scattered a million fireflies across the roof of the world. One evening when there was a full moon he walked Anna to the headland and they stood at the edge of the blowhole and looked out to an ocean lit up in a swathe of silver-white water. Concealed beneath a thicket of she-oaks they embraced on the spiky ground, enveloped in its pungent conifer scent and the sound of the surf, its soft wash against the rocks below.

II

AND SO THEY SETTLE IN, and it seems they have everything they need; everything, that is, except water. If only it would rain. There is a shower one morning early and Luke, who sleeps heavily, quizzes Anna about its duration. 'I didn't hear it,' she says, so he must go and rap against the new fibreglass tank and listen for any increase in the level. As far as he can tell there is none.

They knew about the drought before they came, but this was only a weather report; it was not the same as living, day to day, in the big dry. For the first time they understand what it means to live on the rim of the driest continent, a land of empty rivers that for most of the year, and sometimes for decades, are nothing more than lines on a map, some cartographical promise of a deluge that may or may not arrive. But now here they are; a part of it. The creeks are stony beds and the narrow winding river that feeds the lagoon has shrunk to a muddied stream.

Accustomed to the sub-tropical downpours of the city and the smell of mould in their old apartment, they cannot believe how dry the air is, and how this dryness becomes a part of you, of your skin and hair, and your whole body, and how after a while you crave the feel of moisture in the air, of dampness against your cheek. Soon their tank water begins to smell strange and they send for a filtration system which Luke fits under the sink with surprising deftness. He has turned out to be more practical than Anna imagined.

One evening on a stroll beside the lagoon they come across a handsome, sunburnt man who is fishing for perch with two small children at his side. They strike up a conversation and the fisherman introduces himself as Alan Watts and invites them up to his house on the headland to meet his wife, Bette.

In the weeks that follow they ease into a friendship with the Watts, one that might always have been there in their lives. Alan and Bette belong to that coastal tribe who seem entirely at ease in their sun-ripened bodies and who rarely appear in anything other than shorts and thongs. Anna sometimes jokes to Luke that the Watts' wardrobe must be empty, or used for storing old sporting equipment, but she admires the simplicity of the Watts household; the sparseness of its furniture, the no-frills housekeeping. Bette is a part-time nurse and competition kayaker, an athletic woman with cropped dark hair. Alan is a tall, barrel-chested man in his early forties who teaches maths at the Brockwood High School, in and around the pursuit of his passion for collecting rustic hardware, which he crams into a barn-sized workshop. Both he and Bette are energetic and practical and seem able to do almost anything. A decade ago, before such things were talked about, they built an energy-efficient house with sun walls and solar panels, built it from scratch while they and their two children, Zack and Briony, lived out of a caravan on their block. On a vacant plot next door Alan has tidied up an abandoned tennis court and strung an old fishing net across the middle of its cracked concrete surface. Delighted to find that Luke and Anna can both hit a ball he invites them to play doubles on the weekends, and sometimes of an evening after work. Like all social tennis, it is played with an underlying ferocity, the men volleying at the net as though their life depends on it and swearing under their breath. Nor is Anna immune to this manic athleticism, even if there is something comically grim in the way that Alan barks out the score after every point.

Ten kilometres down the coast is an army base and occasionally a helicopter flies low over the court on a training manoeuvre, materialising from out of the cloud like some jaunty mechanical bird. One late Saturday afternoon a chopper lands on the headland and two young men in uniform get out and stand about chatting under their becalmed rotor blades. Alan can't resist. He breaks off from the tennis and jogs across to say hello. Luke follows at a stroll, not wishing to appear too eager, while the women look at one another and roll their eyes.

Alan introduces himself, and then Luke, and invites the visitors into the Watts' bungalow for a coffee.

'Better not,' says one of the men, amiably. 'We're a bit early.' He looks at his watch. 'We've just got a few minutes to kill.'

'Great spot here,' says the other man. 'I'll bet you get good surf.'

'Not as much as you'd think,' says Alan. 'We get a lot of wind and it can flatten the waves.'

Luke is struck by something. These guys are only a few years younger than I am, he thinks, and yet they make me feel old. He perceives that he is no longer spirited, not in the juiced-up way that these guys are; that he no longer has their youthful sheen, a kind of cocky invincibility. Maybe he never had it. Or maybe he had it and, somewhere in the transition to his thirties, he lost his nerve. Maybe that's why he's come to live in the country. Maybe it wasn't about Anna at all.

Alan, typically, wants to know about the chopper and because he is so friendly and so direct, before long they have learned that at the end of the month one of the crew is off to Afghanistan. 'Well, best of luck,' says Luke, realising that he *is* old, because nothing would induce him to put himself in a place where he might be shot at. Then again, there are things in his life he would die to protect, and with that thought he looks around for the boy, who would surely have been drawn to the mechanical beast. He thinks he catches a glimpse of him lurking in among the shadowy she-oaks that line the court, but no, it's only Zack, skulking after a spat with his sister and searching for lost tennis balls. Luke turns again towards the bluff and gazes wistfully at the crew as they climb back into their machine. The blades begin their whirr, that insistent hypnotic *whoomph,* and the big metal bird rises in a gush of wind, fluttering out over the water towards a pink horizon.

That evening after dinner the two couples play cards. Alan announces that he has rationed the family to two showers a week each and is planning to install a dry lavatory, because flushing is the biggest single use of household water. He is also looking into buying a portable desalinisation plant and running seawater up from the beach to his roof. 'I've downloaded some brochures from the net,' he says, shuffling through a pile of papers at one end of the table.

While the two men are engrossed in these, the women stand at the window, gazing out at a pod of dolphins carousing off the bluff. Bette is not a shy woman but she has a natural reserve so Anna is surprised when she says, 'Do you think, Anna, that you'll ever start a family?'

'We've put that on hold,' says Anna, firmly. 'First we have to decide where home is.' This isn't the whole truth, far from it, and she hopes the boy isn't listening.

In July, Luke's father comes to stay, bringing a case of Margaret River whites and a bottle of

Glenfiddich. Ken is restless and edgy; he has the air of a man on red alert, primed to move in on a problem at a moment's notice. 'Your father is still adjusting to retirement,' Marg had said when she rang to say he was coming. 'He's like a brigadier who's lost his battalion.'

On the first evening Luke takes him for a stroll around the grassy headland. 'There's not much here in the way of facilities, is there?' his father says, tactlessly, gesturing with one of his overlong arms towards the shacks behind the bluff. Ken is a very tall man, and lanky, and it gives him an air of lofty judgement, like a bemused prophet. He has never been at home in the outdoors and he strides towards the Norfolk pines as if an explorer in the New World, part awed and part baffled at how the other half lives. 'You haven't got sick of it yet?'

'It grows on you.' Luke does not want to submit to one of his father's inquisitorial probings. He does not want to get into an argument about his career, about why he does not want to work as a solicitor and has 'wasted' his law degree; about where he is 'going' and whether his superannuation is adequate. The abrasion of his father's implied censure spurs him along at a brisk clip. The sooner they get home and get into the scotch, the better.

'How is Anna's asthma?'

'It's been a lot better, though it's early days yet.'

'Well, that's something,' says Ken, managing to insinuate that from what he's seen so far, the rest of life in Garra Nalla is pretty much nothing. 'And how is she recovering from ...' He pauses, trying to find the words, '... from that other business?'

My God, he can't even name it, thinks Luke in a spasm of bitter scorn. Typical. His father never could deal with the messy human dimension of feeling. But then as he watches the spray foam up from the blowhole, for the first time it occurs to him that the 'other business' must have been painful for Ken, a man with no grandchildren. How helpless he must have felt; an old-fashioned man who took responsibility for everything around him, who felt a duty to protect the weak.

In the days that follow Ken does his best not to appear bored but he doesn't fool Anna. 'He's like an old-fashioned school inspector,' she says to Luke in bed. 'I keep getting the feeling that we're not coming up to scratch. He thinks we've turned into yokels.'

'I hate the way he patronises Gil,' mumbles Luke. He is thinking of that awful false mateyness his father deems it necessary to assume. And Gil with his stiff politeness is almost as annoying.

'You can see they don't like each other.'

'Is it that obvious?'

'It is to me.'

Anna has observed that while Ken is visiting, the boy does not appear, and nor is he to be sighted when Gil is around. Perhaps he doesn't care for older men. But then on the last night of Ken's visit she wakes and thinks that she hears the boy cry-ing. Or has she dreamed it? She gets up and walks to his room at the end of the hallway but the bed is empty. Still, she is not alarmed; she knows that he will return. He always does.

*

Months pass and they move into a difficult spring. It seems that almost every day the winds blow and there will be no spring rain. The drought is one thing, the hectoring wind is another. No-one warned them about the wind. Sometimes on the coast it can bluster for weeks at a time, but this year is worse than any Gil can remember. The surrounding grass, faded to a mustard colour, turns orange at the tips from wind-burn. Even the trees begin to get a crisp look; their canopy is brittle and the undergrowth dried to tinder. On her walks Anna can see that the grasslands are eaten down to bare stubble and grey sandy soil, while the great fortified homestead hovers like a mirage on a plain of shimmering straw. One afternoon a flock of glossy black cockatoos alights on a cluster of she-oaks in the western corner of the yard where they screech in ear-splitting decibels until dusk. When she goes for a walk before dinner, she finds Gil by the near fence, staking his runner beans around an old tyre spoke, and he tells her that the arrival of black cockies is a portent of rain. But the rain doesn't come. Nature is out of whack, thinks Anna; even the birds can't read the signs.

In defiance of the wind she persists in swimming the lagoon so that she can keep up her regular run along the beach to Rittler's Point. Surely the wind must drop soon. But for days, and then weeks, it continues to harass her, blowing in fine swirling gusts so that the sand sticks in her hair and lodges in the crevices of her clothes. Her skin turns to parchment, dried out and stretched tight across her cheekbones in a mask.

'This is getting on my nerves,' she says to Luke. 'Do you realise that bloody wind has howled around here for forty-one days without a break?'

'Forty-*one*?' he asks, wryly.

His detachment is infuriating. It's alright for Luke, the heavy sleeper, but almost every night now *her* sleep is disturbed by the wind gusting against the house; the roof groans and she is woken by the sudden slam of doors along the hallway. Luke never so much as stirs. His head is scarcely on the pillow and he is dead to the world until resurrected at dawn like some bush Lazarus.

One afternoon, foolishly, she hangs the sheets on the line instead of laying them out in the spare room to dry. Instantly they begin to balloon out like galleon sails, flapping violently in the hot gusts that batter the garden. Later, when she walks out to collect the washing, there is a great gap in the line where a white elasticised under-sheet has blown away. She swears, and strides towards the fence to peer through the bushes. Sure enough, there it is on the empty block next door, draped across a patch of bracken like a collapsed parachute. She swears again, because Rodney keeps two pet sheep on this block and their droppings are all through the grass and ferns, and she will have to wash the sheet a second time and water is scarce. She unlatches the gate and the sheep run to her sociably and nuzzle at her hips, trotting behind as she treads roughshod over the brittle ferns. 'Shoo,' she says, as she approaches her washing, 'shoo,' and stoops to lift a corner of the sheet. There, coiled in a perfect whorl, is a black snake with a long, pointed head. And she is frozen. As the clutch of warm cotton falls limply from her hand she begins to back away until, with a shriek, she stumbles backwards onto a pile of stones, grazing her elbow. When at last she reaches the gate, nursing her bloodied elbow, she wrenches the gate open and, half-running, heads for the house. 'Luke!' she shouts at the bottom of the ladder to the attic. Then she opens the fridge, takes out a jug of iced water and pours it over her head. When Luke comes into the kitchen she turns, dripping, towards him. 'Go and get Gil,' she gasps, 'there's a snake in the paddock next door. Under the sheet.'

'What sheet?'

'It blew off the line.'

'I'll get a shovel,' he says.

'No, no, get Gil, he'll know what to do.'

She sinks onto a chair. Now she is shaking. It's not that she has seen a snake, it's that in lifting the sheet she had bent so low, had been so close, had somehow entered into the snake's zone …

When after twenty minutes the two men return, she fusses over Gil, making him a cup of tea, stewed the way he likes it, and buttering some muffins she has defrosted in the microwave. 'Well,' he says, lighting up a cigarette, though he knows she hates the smell of it in the house, 'a copper-head. Your first snake. Now you can call yourself a local.' He winks at Luke, one of those stagey masculine winks that under other circumstances she would find insufferably patronising.

'Bloody wind,' she says.

After a while they stop walking altogether and the canoe lies idle under the veranda. September un-ravels and then October, and still the winds blow and the rains don't come. In the city the weather is just a backdrop to your day, a painted canvas against which you enact the plot of your life. In the country the weather *is* the plot. Sometimes it is overcast and she hopes for precipitation, but before long the sky clears. The clouds return and hang around for days, and you wait, and you wait, and the clouds move on. One morning early she wakes to the surprising sound of thunder. It's coming from the south, and for a long time it rolls on, and on and on in a series of muffled explosions that give rise to hope. Maybe it will move north; maybe at last they will receive the watery benediction they crave. She lies still, hoping to hear something louder, something nearer, but the same remote sound continues on unchanged, rumbling into early dawn to mingle, at last, with the trilling of a blackbird. Then it begins to grow faint and she realises that this dry, hollow thunder is never going to deliver on its promise.

That morning, in exasperation, she emails her sister, Stephanie, in Hong Kong. 'It's hard to describe the effect this weather has on my state of mind,' she writes. 'I don't know if I can stand the drought much longer. I keep wondering if we've made a mistake.'

When she says as much to Luke, he listens patiently. 'Let's give it another year,' he says. 'Weather goes in cycles. It changes all the time.' He puts his arm around her waist appeasingly. 'Come on, Annie, we haven't given it a chance.'

It's alright for him, she thinks; he works with his headphones on, listening to his music, and the rumble of the wind is reduced to mere background noise. Luke always did have a way of blotting out distraction, of drawing the world in around him on his own terms, whereas she seems to bleed out into it, as if she is part of one giant membrane that holds land, sea and sky together. Some days she feels like a fly caught in an invisible web.

Luke is tired of his wife's churlishness. He does not want to think about leaving Garra Nalla. Perhaps one day, but not yet. He jokes with her that he has too much reading to do, that it will take him twelve months at least to read his way through the vicar's books. For a while he has had to put these aside because of a new contract and an overload of work, but tonight he has resumed his acquaintance with Sir Frederick Treves. At last that honest surgeon has arrived in Jerusalem itself: the goal of his pilgrimage, the very heart of his faith. But even here, as elsewhere, he experiences profound disappointment. The famed Via Dolorosa, along which Jesus is said to have carried his cross, is a patent fraud, a *'dirty and callous street'* constructed by merchants for monetary gain. *'Along this route the Stations of the Cross are marked by inscribed stones let into the walks or by other insignia. But the Via Dolorosa is a mere fiction of the Christian Church, a lane of lies . . . The magnitude of the deception can be realized if it be remembered that the site of Calvary is not known, that some forty years after the crucifixion of Christ Jerusalem was so utterly destroyed by Titus as to be left a mass of indistinguishable ruins, that it remained a mere heap of stone for sixty years, and that it was not until some three hundred years after the death of Christ, when every trace of the city of His time had been obliterated, that any attempt was made to discover the so-called sacred sites.'*

What an unedifying spectacle it is to see the worshippers along the way, *'possessed by a delirium of adoration that is morbid and pitiable. They dropped down before the sacred spots like felled cattle. They kissed the stones and moaned and muttered like creatures filled with dread.'*

There is something about Sir Frederick that reminds Luke of his father; that rational scientific mind that wants to believe but is sceptical of everything. He can see his father treading the same path and tut-tutting in the same worldly tone. The well of Mary, the tomb of Lazarus, the Church of the Holy Sepulchre; all have been concocted for the coin of the gullible. As time goes on the all-pervading squalor of his tour seems to induce in Sir Frederick an increasingly acid disillusionment. This dry, stony country, these wretched towns and villages, these gloomy basilicas and their fake relics: can this be the Promised Land?

While Luke reads, the television continues to purr into the late night. Anna is watching CNN and a report on the latest casualties in Iraq. On the screen a black soldier is weeping. 'I just want those guys in Washington to come out and do one day of my rotation with me, one day, do what I do, and I'll willingly serve another fifteen-month rotation if they do that, just come out, one day ...' There is a burning tank, upended, bodies splayed on the road, billowing smoke ... An old Iraqi woman is in her living room, white-haired, in her nightgown, clutching her walking frame and wailing. The American soldiers have dragged a dead civilian in off the road, where they shot him, and onto her small paved terrace, behind a high wall covered in flowering jasmine. Here they are sheltered from snipers, and the old woman is standing bewildered, at her walking frame, surrounded by men in battle dress, one of whom is kneeling over the bloodied civilian corpse and trying frantically to revive it. The camera moves to a close-up of another man sitting on a bench in a shadowy room, to the anguish on the face of this soldier, a captain, handsome, in his late twenties. 'We have six hours out there,' he is saying, and there is a quaver in his voice, 'and six hours off and it's not enough, not enough to wind down, even when we're lying down, when we're supposed to be sleeping, we're in a state of heightened alertness, like permanent, like we're never off ...' Now the camera pans to a bloodied Iraqi soldier who is sitting in the middle of the road, his shredded skin flayed from him by the blast of an explosion. Bystanders have been struck by shrapnel, a tall man in white, bloodied all down one side, is carrying a bleeding child ... a cameraman darts across the road like a whippet ... the soldier in the room again, he is wiping his face with his open hand, over and over. There is nothing on his face to wipe but he keeps on wiping, over and over.

Anna looks down at the boy, who is playing on the rug with some tennis balls. At least, she tells him, you will never have to be a soldier.

One Saturday afternoon, when Luke and Alan Watts are clearing gorse from behind the sandhills, Alan asks after the contents of the vicar's library. 'Do you reckon any of the vicar's books are worth anything? Any first editions?'

'Several, though I doubt their value.' He tells

Alan about Sir Frederick, and his fascination with Treves' account of the Middle East as a torpid terrain on which hardly anything of note ever happens. 'Can you imagine?' he says, hacking away at the wretched yellow weed. 'Look at it now, probably the closest thing ever to a state of permanent war.'

Alan hesitates, and then surprises him. 'Has Gil told you he's got a grandson in Afghanistan?'

'No, he hasn't.' Luke is miffed; he thought Gil told him everything. 'Why wouldn't Gil mention it?'

'I don't know, but he doesn't seem to want to talk about it. Bette found out when his daughter was visiting a few weekends back.'

'How long has his grandson been there?'

'Just a month.'

'What does he do?'

'He's a commando.'

'Is that like the SAS?'

'Similar, but different. Gil said that the SAS are long-range reconnaissance. They go out in small units and basically dig a hole in the ground and live there for days or weeks at a time, observing what's going on around them. If they're sprung they're buggered because they're usually in places where it's difficult if not impossible to retrieve them. Once they've figured out what's going on, they call in the commandos who do the dirty work.'

'Why wouldn't Gil talk about it? He's got strong views about everything else.'

'Bette thinks he's superstitious. You know, if he doesn't dwell on it, then nothing will happen to the boy.'

Luke pauses, his clippers open in mid-air. The boy? He hasn't thought about the boy for quite some time.

But then, on the way home with Alan, he thinks he sees someone who looks like the boy, walking along the dusty road ahead, kicking at stones, his slight figure quivering in the heat.

'Look.'

Alan is standing at the edge of the grassy path, beside the body of a dead swan. It appears to have flown into the wires overhead and been electrocuted, and not all that long ago since there is no sign of it having been set upon by crows. It's a deflating sight: the twisted black carcass, the slash of white feather down its middle, the broken neck splayed at a right angle, the crimson beak lying bright against the sandy stubble of the track.

*

In November the summer heat comes early, and still no sign of rain. Already the days shimmer in the low thirties. Across the paddocks, cracks open in the ground. The air is so dry you can almost hear it crack.

In the weeks that follow it gets hotter, and drier, and still the winds blow. Bush animals begin to roam into the settlement, looking for water. First a sluggish wombat and then a bewildered echidna come to drink from the bird-bath, a lotus-shaped bowl carved from granite. Anna has yet to find a suitable plinth so it rests for now on the ground and this induces her to wonder aloud: if echidnas are on the move, can the snakes be far behind? Any day she expects to look out from across the veranda and see an eastern brown curled around the base of the lotus.

One evening she ventures the hitherto unsayable: what would it take for them to return to the city? For a few hours the wind has dropped and she is sitting in the shade of the veranda. Luke is standing at its edge with his field-glasses, intent on tracking the glide of a white-bellied sea-eagle above the lagoon. Gil said he had once seen a sea-eagle swoop on a black swan, lifting it high into the air in its great talons.

Anna is following the line of Luke's gaze and even without glasses she can see the distinctive contour of the raptor's broad upswept wings. It's not a bird she likes, but she is trying now to sound playful, as if posing a hypothetical question, something to while away the post-dinner lull on a night when there is nothing much on TV. She wants to catch Luke off guard.

'You know, I don't think I could live here all my life,' she says.

Luke doesn't reply. He is watching the eagle as it rises to greater and greater heights. It has caught an air current and is circling upwards in a slow, mesmeric spiral. If he is patient he might be able to track it to its nest, at least if the nest is along the cliff face around Rittler's Point; if it flies home to a tall tree in the hills, then before long it will be lost beyond the range of his field-glasses.

Anna tires of waiting for an answer and gets up from her chair in a huff. Though he gives the appearance of being absorbed in the eagle, Luke is alert to her every movement. He hears the soft rasp of the screen door as it slides along its groove and knows that she has given up on him and retreated into the house.

...

Luke Worley is not a fool. He can see that his wife is in need of a break. When friends in Randwick ring to say that they are about to travel overseas at short notice and ask if Luke and Anna would be interested in house-sitting, he feigns enthusiasm. 'Let's take some time off and go to town,' he says. 'We can stock up on things, go to a club, see a few people. You can stay on longer if you like and work on the laptop. Gil will water the garden while we're away.'

'I wish they had given us more notice,' she says, but he knows this is only token resistance.

On the following Friday they pack up and drop the keys into Gil.

'Back to the city, eh?' he says. 'Better watch out or you might get caught there.'

'Don't worry about that,' says Luke.

At the turn-off to the freeway he looks back at the windswept headland of Garra Nalla and the glinting roof of what is now their home. This is our Promised Land, he thinks, and we are here to stay.

On the drive along the coast he is buoyant,

and looking forward, even, to the change. But almost from the moment they begin to unpack in the small high-rise apartment in Bondi Junction he is irritable and censorious. 'At least you'll be in striking distance of the water,' his friends had said. Striking distance? What did that mean? An overpopulated Bondi where even the gulls seem brazen and acquisitive?

'Gulls are gulls, Luke,' says Anna as they stroll along the boulevard on a Sunday morning.

'Not when they're used to a diet of chips and souvlaki.' He thinks of the Pacific gulls at home, fossicking at low tide for cockles; how they rise up over the shallows and hover above the reef, the better to drop their prey on the rocks below so that the shells can smash and disgorge their meat.

Five days in and Luke returns to the coast. The night before his departure they dine with friends in a noisy Thai restaurant in Newtown where he is prickly and distant, complaining of the noise and making a show of not being able to hear anything said to him. On the drive home

Anna is silent and in the morning she is relieved to see him go. Nothing pleases him, whereas for her it's enough to be out of the wind. It's true that right now it is windy in the city, but there are more interesting places to escape it. Even if the air is fouled with exhaust fumes and the nights are broken with sirens, there is much here that is sensual and exciting, and not all of it in neon. She loves the lurid metropolitan sunsets, and she cannot see how these flushed and burnished skies are inferior to what they look out on from the veranda at Garra Nalla; indeed, the dark, block-ish shapes of the city skyline, the contrast of their sharp-edged silhouettes against a fiery sky, confer on nature an even greater drama.

But then, somewhere in the middle of the second week she begins to feel claustrophobic. She misses her house, its many rooms; the wide veranda; the great glittering expanse of the lagoon; the feeling of gliding across the water in their canoe. And she misses the she-oaks with their wispy canopies that seem to hum and vibrate in the heat. Damn Luke, damn his stupid ideas. All he has succeeded in doing is creating a situation where she doesn't feel at home anywhere. Now she belongs in neither place, like some migratory bird that has lost its bearings. But the most disturbing thing is this: here in the city there has been no sign of the boy. At night she wills him to come and lie beside her on the wide, king-sized futon; she wants to stroke her palm along the golden sheen of his forehead, to study the way his dark eyelashes curl against his cheek. She longs to see him in the tiny kitchen of the apartment, sitting up at the table with his spoon clasped at a languid angle as he knocks his foot rhythmically against the leg of his chair. But when she wakes in the dark she is alone; in her mind's eye she can see him in the old farmhouse, clattering around the veranda or lost in the swinging fold of the hammock. Why, she asks herself, does he always have to side with his father? Or could it be that she is losing her power to summon him? In a panic she realises that it's been three weeks since he last came to her and now when she thinks of his face it is pale and slightly out of focus.

On her last day in the city she buys a book on coastal vegetation and sits in the courtyard of a coffee shop in Darlinghurst, sketching a plan for a garden of bush rosemary and casuarinas. Quietly, she has resolved to give it another year in Garra Nalla. This is not too much to ask, it is what they agreed at the outset, after all those nights of debating the move in their Glebe apartment. But secretly she has made up her mind: they must go. One day. In the meantime she will work on leaving something worthwhile behind. She needs a project, and since the winds are eroding the topsoil of her garden it makes sense to plant more trees. And of all trees, the casuarinas are her favourite. Here, for once, nature is on her side. According to her book, these hardy pines are the great coastal survivors; resistant to salt and wind and minimal in their water needs, they are able to grow fast in poor soils. Better still, they attract the birds. There is a big bush nursery outside of Brockwood and when she returns she will drive there and buy as many varieties as she can find, but especially the *Allocasuarina*, or weeping she-oak.

These are the most seductive trees of all, mysterious trees, like wraiths, with long filaments that resemble quills and a subtle palette of foliage that is neither blue nor green nor grey nor rusty brown but all of these melding into a mystical blur.

The *Allocasuarina*, she discovers, has two distinct forms, male and female. The male tree has long reddish tips at the end of its fine, needle-like branches and these pollinate the rust-red globes of flower on the female tree. Sometimes, says her book, the production of pollen can be so prolific that a reddish carpet is strewn around the ground beneath, and she has seen this on her walks along Rittler's Point. But best of all, she loves the sound of the wind in the she-oaks at night, the way the canopy sways and sings in an eerie whistle that might be unnerving if it were not so beguiling.

Luke is waiting with Gil to collect her at the Brock-wood station. They have been to the hardware store to buy materials for a snake-proof fence and with their wiry bodies and broad-brimmed hats they look like two old stockmen, whiling away time on the platform.

'I wouldn't plant she-oaks,' says Gil, when she tells him of her plan.

'Why not?'

'Because they burn like buggery. Light up like a Christmas tree. Get a fire in these parts and they'll endanger your house.'

'So what do you plant?'

'They say one of the pittosporums is the most resistant but I've never grown 'em.'

This is typical of the locals, she thinks, huffily. Full of a wisdom they seldom act upon. That night she trawls the net in search of further knowledge and finds that the casuarina is indeed a fireweed. It burns hot in a spangled dance of embers and is reborn from a white bed of ash. *'Some Australian species respond to fire as others do to rain,'* she reads, and the casuarina is one of them. *'There are instances of species, thought extinct, that fire freed from a near-fatal dormancy.'* Australia, it seems, is a land of phoenix trees: fertile in extremity.

...

One evening, Gil comes over to the house in an agitated state. He has been out walking in the wind and there are small twigs and dried leaves caught in his hair so that he looks like a scarecrow, or a figure from a fable. It's clear that he is angry – more than that, incensed – for he has just heard that the consortium is soon to begin work on a vast tree plantation. The sheep are to be sold off and the grasslands will be ploughed into furrows for saplings, row after row of blue-gums, laid out in straight lines that will run all the way down to the lagoon. They will scour the land with bulldozers and then the spray trucks will come with their pale green tanks of poison and the men in their fluorescent orange jackets will walk the furrows with their rods of pesticide, and when it does rain, as eventually it must, the chemicals will wash out of the soil and foul the lagoon. The settlement of Garra Nalla will be surrounded on three sides by a toxic geometry of straight lines: an insult to Nature; a hideous symmetry.

'In the middle of a bloody drought!' fumes

Gil. 'It'll be a fire hazard for one thing. And I'll tell you another thing. It'll suck up all the water out of the water table and eventually out of the lagoon. In five years' time that lagoon will be a bloody mudflat. Them swans'll have to find somewhere else to breed.'

'How dare they!' exclaims Anna. 'How dare they come in and violate this place! What about the council? Aren't there any planning guidelines?'

'The council!' exclaims Gil. 'They're in the bloody pockets of the developers, always have been, always will be!'

Anna is distraught. What is the point of this rural idyll if they are at the mercy of the consortium? Luke, too, is unsettled by this news, at least for a time, but after a few days he seems able to shrug it off, to imply that she is taking it too personally. There it is again, that infuriating detachment. See, she says to the boy. See, he doesn't *deal* with things. But the boy skitters away from her and out to the veranda. True to form, he remains loyal to his father.

In the weeks that follow Anna begins to resent her husband. When she saw his fine, expressive face at the train station she had quickened with desire. How right he always looked; how loose-limbed and at ease. How perfectly proportioned his body, the same figure as his father and yet without Ken's stony awkwardness. No matter what he said, or how greatly he exasperated her, it was always disarming, this indefinable grace Luke had. But now it is not enough. For what kind of cul-de-sac has he led them into? He came here out of his protectiveness towards her, but now it seems that he has become complacent, has lost all ambition. No wonder his father is concerned. One of the things she has always admired about Luke is that he is, well, sharp; not just his thin, angular body and the short, spiky hair, but a cast of mind that sees through bullshit and gets to the point of everything fast. At least, this is how he used to be. Now he goes about with a happily bemused expression on his face, like he's stoned, or sits cross-legged on the veranda drinking wine with Rodney. Yesterday she overheard them having an inane conversation about crows. Rodney spoke of a rare sighting on his property in the hills of the Hobby, a small but deadly falcon with slate blue wings, able to fly at great speed and catch its prey on the wing, and she listened as he described, almost gloatingly, how he had watched it 'take out' a parrot. 'Awesome.'

Luke sat up in his chair, excited. 'Haven't seen a falcon round here,' he said. 'If he comes again, ring me.'

'Why? By the time you got there, it'd be gone. Anyway,' said Rodney, 'why is it that nobody loves the old crow? He's only a scavenger, he doesn't kill other birds.'

'Yeah, but he's dead common,' said Luke.

'My old man used to say that the only thing a crow's good for is target practice, not that you can kill one of the buggers.'

'How do you mean?' asked Luke.

'Never seen anyone manage to shoot a crow, not shoot it dead. You hit the bloody thing, feathers puff in all directions and the crow flies off.' Rodney gave his hoarse smoker's chuckle and Luke grinned inanely as if he'd just been let in on some tremendous joke. He had an expression on his face she had never seen before, like an idiot boy.

One afternoon, looking out the kitchen window, she observes his stringy figure meandering up the drive, his face wearing a dreamy, abstracted look. Around his neck hang the two objects that accompany him on all his walks, his field-glasses and his USB memory stick, and there is something strange about him, something beyond her. At that moment she falls into a spiral of panic; it is as if she is encountering a stranger. She finds she is looking at her husband in an almost impersonal way, as though at a figure in the landscape, or one of those birds he is always gazing at. Perhaps that's all any of them are, figures in a landscape. In each era new figures come, others go, but the land remains and their sense of ownership is an illusion, a mirage brought on by too many days in the hot sun. So what is this pointless dance that they are engaged in, this dance where they whirl together in an endless circle, locked in the illusion that they are going somewhere, that what they do has meaning beyond their own day-to-day survival? At any moment they could disappear from this place and nothing would change, nothing of consequence, so vast is the land and so small are they. And the thought of this brings on a rush of vertigo, a dizzying sense of disorientation, as if she is about to fall, but that when she falls she will be weightless. She has lost her roots, her anchorage to the earth; she might float away into the blue of the sky and never be heard from again. When, finally, Luke walks through the door she wants to run to him, to clutch at him and steady herself. Perhaps it's to do with the boy, for it feels like he's abandoned them. Since she returned from the city he eludes her; she sees him nowhere, and this is making her unhinged. The world is spinning away from her. Something is dying, something is leaching away from them; some once vivid hue in the inner landscape of her consciousness is beginning to fade.

III

On the last Saturday in November Anna and Luke set out for the Brockwood nursery to buy she-oaks, accompanied by the Watts, who have suggested they detour into the hills to have lunch at the Wolga hotel, newly painted and restored with wide verandas and intricate wrought-iron railings. Tables are set out in the shade of the upstairs veranda and the food is good. There is no wind in the hills and for those few hours Anna feels she might almost regain her old equilibrium.

On the following Sunday, a day of baking heat, they plant their new saplings, venturing out in mid-morning with a bundle of stakes and the sheet of paper on which Anna has sketched her plan. Over breakfast Luke had remarked teasingly on the care she has taken to design a seemingly random layout that she hopes will create a true bush effect, a kind of formless beauty. She has put so much thought into the form of the formless, he says, but 'a garden is a garden. It can never be the bush.'

'I know,' she replies, good-naturedly, 'but we can meet the bush halfway.'

Afterwards they celebrate with Gil and the Watts, who join them for a long lunch of barbecued fish and the last two bottles of Margaret River white left over from Ken's visit. The wind has dropped and they take this as a good omen, though the harsh light corrals them in the shade of the veranda.

Around four the visitors leave and Luke takes his wife by the arm and leads her into the house. There, in a shaded corner of the living room, they make love on the old bush settle, then rise languidly and return to the veranda to lie dozing on the cane lounges.

Late in the afternoon, Anna opens her eyes to

find that the sky above her, a washed-out blue, is mottled with brown smudge. Beyond the yellow grasslands a cloud of smoke is billowing up from behind the hills.

Luke sits up and yawns. 'Looks like a bushfire,' he says.

She raises a hand to shade her eyes, trying to get a fix on where the smoke is coming from. It appears to be rising from deep ravines in the western ranges, a vast acreage of crown land that recedes into the interior. Meanwhile the smoke cloud is expanding, seeping out into the sky like a release of octopus ink.

'I don't like the look of that,' she says.

'Don't worry. It's a long way away.'

The gate creaks and it's Alan, returning to retrieve Bette's sunglasses. He gestures in the direction of the smoke. 'That's a hell of a conflagration they've got going back there.'

'Burning off?'

'Hard to say. I did see a Forestry chopper flying over a few days ago. Might have dropped one of those canisters they use to start a back-burn.'

Anna frowns. 'I'm glad we live near the water.'

Alan is lifting the cushions on the veranda, looking for Bette's glasses. 'It wouldn't be the first fire we've had in these parts,' he says. 'They never reach the coast.'

In the morning, when they wake, the bedroom reeks of burning eucalypt: pungent, sweet and weirdly intoxicating. Luke sits bolt upright, sniffing the air, then climbs out of bed to stand naked by the window. Raised up on one elbow Anna can see what he sees, a fug of pale grey smoke that blankets the landscape like winter fog, so dense they can only just make out the contours of Gil's bungalow below them. It's as if they are marooned. 'The fire must be a long way away,' says Anna, for she can see no flame, only the ghostly grey outline of the hills.

After breakfast Luke checks the temperature gauge on the veranda and already it stands at thirty-four. When Anna walks out into the garden the haze is thick and acrid and she is curious as to whether it will bring on her asthma. What if she were to have a seizure? In the linen cupboard they keep a nebuliser machine but she has not had to use it since they got here. Still, when she returns to the house she checks that the small plastic ampoules of Salbutamol are up to date.

By noon the house is stifling. All morning they have sat at their work-stations with the ceiling fans on full, but the futile whirr of the rotor blades does nothing to relieve their clammy discomfort. While she waits for her coffee to brew, Anna puts her head under the tap and rinses her singlet top in the basin so that it clings wetly to her skin. Her hair is slicked back behind her ears and the drips slide onto her shoulders and down into the crevice of her breasts. 'I feel like a wet flannel,' she says to Luke, who is working on his laptop at the kitchen table because the attic room is an oven. Every now and then he gets up and goes to the window but it's impossible to see anything. The smoke is too thick.

In the late afternoon he drives to collect their mail and returns looking unhealthily flushed, his eyes red. 'I just checked the gauge,' he says. 'It's thirty-nine on the veranda.'

Darkness falls and they sit under the ceiling fan in the kitchen and eat a supper of cold chicken salad. Then they climb the let-down ladder to Luke's attic, the better to see the fires burning in the hills. The eerie smoke pall that settled over-night has blown away and now for the first time they can see the flames, zig-zagging lines of flickering orange that look like the lighted streets of cities. And they stand at the window for a long time, because of the queer beauty of it, and because of how enthralling it is to watch a whole mountain range burn. First comes the plume of black smoke, rising up from behind the ridges and lit with a dirty orange light. The flames in the ravines, not yet visible, reflect upwards into a murky glow that hovers above the silhouette of the highest peak. Then with breathtaking speed the flames come racing over the summit, flaring on either side of its rocky face. Along the white ribbon of road that winds into the hills, tiny fire-trucks, like toys, can be seen hurtling towards the front, their fixed lights blinking in a steady pulse.

At last they climb downstairs and prepare for bed, showering under a tepid trickle from the tanks. Mundane tasks like cleaning teeth take on a new weight. The air seems freighted with portent. Mentally they try to shrug it off; this is silly, and the fires are a long way to the west. Still, they sleep fitfully, limbs splayed across clammy sheets. Anna wakes around three and gets up to look out and check on the red glow in the hills. The moon is a hazy crescent and she has not seen the boy in weeks, not even a glimpse, not on the veranda, not in the canoe, nor in the garden or his bed. It's a long time since she heard his stick clatter along the veranda, and now there is a fire burning on the rim of their world. Where are you? she asks. Is it something we've done, some oversight in our thoughts? Have we become too self-absorbed and careless? Have you decided, after all, to leave us? And the thought of this brings on a hollow sick feeling, and she crouches on the edge of the sofa, in the dark, and weeps, hoping that Luke will

wake, will come and comfort her. But Luke is a
heavy sleeper and she must sit through the night
and bear this alone. At last, as dawn breaks along
the eastern curve of the headland and the she-
oaks are outlined in shadow against a pinkish yellow sky, she is spent from weeping, and hungry.
She gets up to make tea and toast and as she pot-
ters around in the half-light of the kitchen she is
comforted by the homeliness of this room. What
a consoling space it is, with its sturdy iron stove,
even if for weeks now it has been too hot to light
and they have used the electric hotplates. She lifts
the lid of the wood-box; there are still a few neatly
cut logs stacked to one side and the sight of their
splintery weft is reassuring. She rinses her cup
and plate in the sink, and returns to bed to fall
into a limp, dreamless sleep.

When she wakes, Luke is standing over her
with a mug of steaming tea. He has been up since
six, listening to the radio. 'The fires have reached
the foothills,' he says. 'We need to take precautions.' She gets up and goes across to the window.
Vast swathes of smoke are billowing up from the

foothills but she can see the fire-trucks are there, and the radio tells them that earth-movers have been mobilised to cut a series of fire breaks.

'What kinds of precautions?' she asks.

Beside her muesli bowl is a printed sheet. Luke has downloaded a guide to fire prevention and from this he has compiled a checklist which they study over breakfast. By nine they are ready to set about their tasks. Anna begins by filling the claw-footed bath and stacking a pile of towels beside it. Luke fills their plastic buckets and sets them down by the front and back doors. Out in the hot, smoky air, thick with grit and swirling litter, he drags the hose to the empty wheelie bin and rests the nozzle against the edge, leaving the bin to fill while he unlocks the garage and carries the ladder out to prop against the side of the house. When the wheelie bin is full he climbs the ladder and sets to work clearing the guttering. In his pockets are old walking socks rolled into tight balls and when he has finished with the guttering he will use these to block the downpipes.

Anna has neglected to put on a hat and soon a

fine black soot settles over her skin. Blinded by grit she stumbles into the house to fill a cup with warm water and as she leans over the sink to dribble it into her eyes she hears the radio go dead. Outside again, she shouts up at Luke atop the ladder: 'The power is off!'

'The fire must have burnt out the power station in the hills,' he says. And it occurs to them both that without electricity to power the pumps on their tanks they will be helpless to defend the house. Still, the fire is some distance away. The thing to do is to get on and rake up the bush litter from around the property. Reluctantly Anna removes the mulch she had placed around her she-oak saplings just a few days before, shovelling it into a hessian bag while Luke takes the hedge clippers to a stand of dried-out bamboo.

'This smoke is getting thicker,' he says at last, breathing heavily and letting the clippers drop to the ground. 'I'm going down to Gil's to see what's happening.'

'I'll come with you.'

'You should stay out of the smoke.'

'It's not affecting me. Really.' But she takes a silk scarf, wets it under the tap and ties it around her nose and mouth. Then she slips her inhalant into her pocket.

A big swell is breaking in over the rocks and by now the air is a heady mix of smoke and salt. They find Gil in the kitchen frying sausages over a single gas ring. The rear porch and back wall of his cottage are overgrown with vines so that the kitchen is like a dark cave and the flame on the gas ring glows unnaturally bright.

'Ever seen anything like this before?' asks Luke.

'Never. I'd hate to be up in them hills.'

'Do you need a hand with anything?'

'Don't worry about me.' He pokes a charcoaled sausage. 'We've had fires in the hills before. They never reach the coast.'

Back at the house they prepare an omelette on their own gas ring and eat it with bread and beer that is still cold. Then they light up a packet of candles left in a cupboard by the previous owner and settle in for the night. Luke sits cross-legged on a cushion on the floor with two wrought-iron candelabra on either side of his knees, enough light to read by. After a long break he has returned to reading Sir Frederick Treves' account of his pilgrimage to Palestine. When he returned from Sydney he took the book down from the shelf and began again where he had left off, for the story haunts him and he wants after all to know how the journey ends. Will Sir Frederick find the meaningful consolation for his daughter's death that has so far eluded him, some revelation at the heart of the Holy Land?

Luke reads for an hour, waiting for a turn in events, though it seems that Sir Frederick is destined for disenchantment. But then, in the very last pages he arrives finally at a place that does not disappoint him. And it's not Nazareth, it's not Bethlehem, nor even is it Jerusalem; no, it's the fragrant city of Damascus, *the oldest city in the world*. The road in, he writes, is a *delectable* passage through outlying vineyards, orange groves, orchards of pomegranates and fields of new corn, through rustling walnut trees and gardens of sun-bleached roses. There are shady walks and reedy pools that link a network of small, peaceful villages until, finally, the traveller arrives at the walls of the city and the gateway of the great Khan. *'There is some romance about the beginning of things: there is even a deeper sentiment about their ending. Here is the goal of the caravan, the end of the journey. Day after day, for weary weeks, the one object clear in the eyes of every tired man on the march is the gateway of the Khan of Damascus, the great inn or caravanserai of the city. Here at this gateway is a place where things end, and within it the shadow of great peace.'* There is more from Sir Frederick in this vein, lyrical descriptions of domestic courtyards with fountains and flowering gardens glimpsed along the way, of all-night bazaars lit by lamplight, of Damascus as *'a city of dreams'*. And how odd this is, for isn't Sir Frederick a Christian? And yet the first encampment in which he finds himself happy – beyond even this, inspired – is a citadel of Islam. It appears to Luke that despite his stern low-church principles, Treves has fallen in love with the city's exotica, and especially the Great Bazaar where he and his wife are intoxicated by the perfumeries. '*The gardens of Damascus are full of roses; the damask rose takes its name from the city, while among the strange and ancient things still manufactured in the town is attar of roses. As my wife and I wished to purchase some of this perfume, we were taken by the dragoman to a certain merchant in the great bazaar who was to be found in a fragrant corner of that splendid labyrinth.*' Luke adjusts his position on the floor; his legs are beginning to cramp and his right foot is going to sleep. A gust of wind blows down the chimney and the candles flicker wildly. Still, he likes the candlelight; there is a lambent peace in this, a softly illuminated slowing of time.

Anna works with her laptop on her knees. She writes to her sister in Hong Kong, imagining Stephanie in her apartment tower and overlooking the glittering harbour while they are here in the smoking bush without water or electricity. But she does not envy her sister; the glow of the candlelight makes her strangely content. 'There is a bushfire in the hills,' she writes, 'but it seems unreal. I suppose we ought to feel terrified but instead we feel calm. Perhaps it's because we are by the sea and just a short sprint to the water.'

But later that night, sitting on the edge of the bed, her mood darkens and she is seized by a spasm of fear mixed with indignation. What if the fires in the foothills sweep across the grasslands tomorrow? What if they reach the coast? And what about this house? It has only been theirs for such a short time. Are they never to have a home? And what, if anything, would be left after a fire? She begins to rub moisturiser into her throat and suddenly her hand is trembling and her familiar night rituals seem absurd. The threat of loss is beginning to chew at her mind like a small, gnawing rodent and when she turns out the light it's a long time before, exhausted, she drifts into a fretful and vivid dream. She is living upstairs in a rickety wooden building that looks like a decrepit department store. The upper balcony is alight and already flames are flickering along the mezzanine balustrade. Downstairs there are rooms crammed with her possessions, things she didn't know she had: antique wall tapestries, bead-encrusted cushions, intricately wrought chairs that are thickets of cast-iron. A large open cupboard is stuffed with neatly folded linen, layer upon layer of embossed tablecloths. And the flames are burning nearer, the upper balcony close to collapse, yet she continues to rummage through the bric-à-brac. Ah, but where is the boy? She had almost forgotten him. Where could he possibly be? Is he hiding again, playing his childish games? Luke is standing in the doorway, clutching suitcases in each hand. Hurry up, he says, we have to get out of here, we have to get out of here *now*. But what about the boy, she groans, we can't go without him, we can't leave him behind —

She wakes in a prickly sweat, and her heart is lurching in her chest. The fact that she can hear it pounding makes her suddenly aware of the stillness outside. It's first light and the wind has dropped. Relief, at last! She goes out to the kitchen and Luke is there, frying bacon over the gas ring and listening to their battery radio. 'They've issued a full alert for tomorrow for the towns along the coast,' he says. 'That's us.'

'What do we do?'

'Pack a suitcase and put it by the door.'

'But the wind has dropped.'

'Not for long. The forecast is for hot nor'-westerlies in the afternoon.'

Over breakfast they listen to radio bulletins, which by now are being relayed every half hour. The small town of Wolga in the hills, where they drove with the Watts only the Sunday before, has been incinerated and the historic hotel where they ate lunch razed to its blackened stumps. More worryingly, a second front has broken out on the coast, though it is several kilometres to the north of Garra Nalla. To reach them it would have to burn down through a long strip of bush reserve that ends at the northern tip of their settlement, and this would take days. From the north, at least, the wind is in their favour, and although the highway to the north is closed, the fire is moving slowly.

Around ten in the morning, Alan rings. 'Bette's a bit jittery,' he says. 'She can't decide whether to drive the kids south or keep them here.'

'What do you think?' asks Anna.

'I've told her it's always risky to drive in a fire and they're better off here with their backs to the sea. I think she needs something to take her mind off it so I suggested a game of tennis.'

He can't be serious. 'Alan wants to play tennis,' she mouths to Luke, raising her eyebrows and pulling a face.

'Why not?' he says. 'Better than sitting around waiting.'

It's an odd sensation to play with the sky overhead a brown pall of smoke. A helicopter flies low over the court, only this time it's a Forestry chopper, and they look up and wave. A light ash rains on their skin; it settles in the creases of their clothes while the grit leaves a bitter coating on their teeth. Behind them, on the Watts' deck, Briony and Zack cavort around an old soccer table, shrieking and whooping and spinning the long metal rods with such manic intensity that the fixed plastic dolls go rattling into a blur. We're all mad, thinks Anna, as she walks to the baseline to serve, and with her back to the others she removes her asthma puffer from her pocket and takes two furtive indrawn breaths.

With only six games played they are spent. Exhausted by the heat and sodden with sweat they go home to shower. After lunch they congregate on the headland and from here, for the first time, they can see signs of the coastal fire burning towards them from the north. Against the horizon is a pale grey smoke plume that wasn't there yesterday, while black smoke is billowing up from a distant promontory. Luke has brought his field-glasses and they take it in turns to focus on the burning sandhills, on the low, lazy flames flickering among clumps of marram grass.

There is nothing to do but to go home and wait. Luke resumes his work on the laptop, but Anna is restless. She needs a task, a manual task, something with a lot of chopping and slicing and shredding, and she sets to work on a coleslaw.

In mid-afternoon, the hot nor'westerlies blow in. A strange light settles over the paddocks and the sky turns a dull greyish yellow. The trees in the garden begin to whip violently and the house shudders. Anna finds it impossible to settle, but Luke sits for more than an hour at the kitchen table, tapping away at his laptop while the wind churns and churns through the garden and the river wattles thrash at the windows, their leaves rasping against the glass in a frenzy. From time to time the roof booms in a convulsion of iron and the old doors rattle on their hinges.

By late afternoon the winds have risen in intensity to a roar. It's a throttling, metallic sound and the rattling of tin and flapping of corrugated iron play on Anna's nerves. Even Luke is spooked.

'This is bad,' he says, 'it must be a hundred and forty ks an hour.'

Impossible, she thinks.

'I'm going up to the headland,' he says.

'You can't go out in this wind.'

'I need to see what's happening. I need to get oriented.'

'Wait for me.'

'Anna, you can't be serious. What if your breathing is affected?'

'I told you, it's not happening. I'm okay.'

Impatiently he hovers by the back door while she winds a silk scarf around her nose and mouth and looks for her wraparound sunglasses. Then, with shoulders braced, they hurl their bodies forward up the hill, staggering into the wind like drunks. As they walk they can see a cluster of townspeople already standing on the headland, tottering in the strong gusts and shielding their eyes with cupped palms. Gil is there, alongside Alan, and both are staring out to the northern end of the lagoon, to the rocky outcrop of Rittler's Point. The sky above the western foothills is lit with a great wall of flame and a mass of greyish white smoke is being blown out towards the sea. At the bottom of the foothills lie the grasslands, grazed to a stubble, except for where they are bisected by a long narrow corridor of bush, and it is here that a spot fire has taken hold and is raging towards the highway and the trees behind Rittler's Point.

Within minutes the fire has jumped the road and the bush at the rear of the point is rent with great orange flares. Anna opens her mouth to speak and can only gasp for she knows there are houses concealed in among those trees. 'Jesus, look at that,' whispers Luke, his breath hot on her neck as they watch the outline of a roof dissolving into smoke and flame. At that moment the point erupts with a deafening boom. Trees are exploding into fire-bombs and great shards of burning bark are being flung into the air and out to sea. Even here, across the lagoon, the air is vibrating from the explosive force of the firestorm, while all around them, small black embers are swirling and gliding on anarchic currents of air. And now the sandhills are alight, the flames from the boobialla rearing up into a rapidly darkening sky. More and more embers are flying out to sea, so far out that the watchers are filled with dread, for the wind is driving the flames towards them, and with such force that there is no way that the fire won't jump the lagoon.

People have begun to come and go, returning in boots and woollen clothing and carrying rakes. The afternoon is dim, the sun obscured; the only light emanates from the wall of flame that burns along the rim of the foothills and the hissing snake-fire in the dunes. From time to time an errant gust hurls a shard of burning bark across the lagoon and someone takes to it frenziedly with a bough or rake.

For an hour they watch their sandhills burn, standing around like useless sentinels. Then Gil, who has been looking out with his arms folded and his hat jammed down low over his eyes, turns to the others and points. 'The wind's changed,' he says. 'It's turned around.' And they see that this is so, that the fire in the sandhills is burning now on the lee side of the wind and that the flames are burning upright. No longer driven by the wind, they struggle against it, their progress slowed and visibly slackening.

'That fire's not going to jump that lagoon now, not against the wind,' says Gil. He turns to Luke. 'With luck, we might have seen the worst of it.' He cups his hands and shouts down to Alan, who, along with a dozen others, has stationed himself at the edge of the lagoon, in wait for flying embers. 'The wind's turned!'

Alan looks up and nods. 'I know,' he shouts back, 'but we still need to keep a lookout.'

'I'll stay,' offers Luke. 'I don't know if I could sleep tonight while those sandhills are burning.'

'Me neither,' says Gil. 'There's a few of us can hang around, we can keep up a bit of a roster.'

It's then that Bette gives a sharp cry and points away from the dunes to the northern sky behind them. 'Look!' When they turn they see for the first time that a monstrous cloud of smoke is surging towards them from the north. So intent have they been on the fire on the southern beach that in the near darkness they have paid no heed to their rear. But now the smoke cloud from the north is billowing out over the coastal reserve like a looming squall line, except this is not a storm cloud, and there is something different about it, something incandescent and alive. Within its dark, surging mass there are orange flecks and glimmers and its lower rim is lit by a golden corona of flame. This can mean only one thing: the very air is alight.

Alan jabs his rake into the sand. 'What the fuck is *that*?'

'It looks like it might be blowing in from the northern front,' says Gil. 'But that's miles up the coast, surely to Christ it wouldn't have got here already —' He stops in mid-sentence. A yellow and red fireball is unravelling from the black underbelly of the smoke cloud. In one incandescent arc it catapults high over the paddocks, across the freeway and down into the bush at the edge of the settlement. In an instant the canopy explodes into flame.

'Holy shit!' Almost in one breath the watchers beside the lagoon break into a run. Alan is yelling

ahead to Bette. 'Take the kids to the beach. Wait on the rocks!'

'You go with her,' says Luke to Anna. Already, half-blinded by smoke, they are sprinting along the road.

'No,' she says, and he is not inclined to argue further for they have reached the bottom of the driveway to their house. Anna flings open the back door and they head for the bedroom to scrabble in the wardrobe for woollen clothes. Luke takes out his heaviest sweater, an old favourite in thick navy-blue rib, but after contemplating it for a few seconds tosses it onto the bed. Anna wishes that she had taken up Luke's suggestion and bought a wide-brimmed akubra instead of mocking his own purchase ('cowboy!') earlier in the year. The windows are already secured and she runs to the bathroom and plunges the entire pile of towels beside the bath into its lukewarm water, wringing them out and rolling them into thick ropes that she can jam against the doors. Through the window she can see Luke in the garden. As he strides toward the back fence, wet sugar-bag in hand, the red-gum beside the garage gives off a great crackling *whoosh* and dissolves into a column of flame.

The speed with which the fire-ball engulfs them is something they will later replay in their heads, over and over, because it is scarcely credible. One minute the squall line of cloud, the next a maelstrom of smoke and flaming embers hurtling into the backyard. Luke runs towards the nearest of these and begins to beat at it in a fury. The noise of the wind is infernal; within its incendiary metallic roar he can hear the ferment of the trees, their hiss and crackle as they combust into a firestorm. A geyser of white-hot cinders sprays above the fence line like a giant Roman candle and he sees that the side gate is alight, only a few metres from the veranda. Anna, too, has spotted this. She opens the door, bucket in hand, and in that moment a great tidal wave of flame comes roaring up through the she-oaks behind the top fence.

'Get back inside!' Luke dives for the door and slams it shut behind them.

For a moment they stand there, gaping at each other in horror. It's too late now to run for the rocks. The fire has swept around to their right and they have no clear path to the beach. They could take a circuitous route to the left but who knows what lies on the other side and what if they take a wrong turn and are trapped? Through the window they can see flames licking at the wooden steps to the veranda and Luke is about to run out with the hessian bag when she pulls at his arm. 'Listen,' she says. In all the din they can hear a new sound, the hum of an engine. From out of the smoke that obscures their drive-way a red fire-truck emerges, reversing up to the edge of the veranda and flattening a bed of pink geraniums. A squat figure in a bright yellow fire suit and white helmet jumps from the truck just as Luke opens the back door. The firey pushes up his visor and beckons them both towards him. 'Get in the truck!' he yells. They run to the passenger side and clamber on top of the second fireman, who shrinks back in his seat to accommodate them, and incredibly the fire is sucked in through the open door so that flames dart into the cabin. As the young firey yanks at the door the truck is already hurtling forward and jammed together in a fug of soot and sweat, scarcely able to breathe, they throttle down the smoke-filled driveway, flames leaping at the windows and racing them to the turn-off. Luke can only stare as the stickers on the wind-screen peel away into tight curls while the side mirror on the truck begins to melt and buckle out of shape. Thank God the driver had the fore-sight to back in, he thinks; they would never have had time to turn.

Taking his bearings from the Norfolk pines on the bluff, barely visible in the smoke, Luke guides the driver to the turning circle beside the lagoon. There, breathless, they sit limply, shoulder to shoulder, hearts pounding in the fetid cabin. The driver is a solid man with a pro-truding gut and he is heaving. He flings open the cabin door, steps down heavily and comes around to the passenger side where Luke and Anna have spilled out onto the gravel, mumbling apologies to the young firey they have almost fallen over and whose name they still don't know. 'Best to stay by the water for now,' says the driver. His voice is raw, his face streaked with grimy sweat. And then, as Luke turns to thank him: 'Are you lucky or what?' he croaks. 'We didn't know you were there. We drove in to get away from the front. Big mistake. Or could have been.'

Luke nods. 'Thanks,' he says, 'and good luck,' and in a quick, instinctive gesture the two men shake hands. The firey clambers back into the truck and accelerates off down the road, disappearing into what is now premature night.

In the gloom of smoke haze that obscures the lagoon, Anna recognises many of the locals. Almost everyone has waded waist deep into the water to escape the radiant heat and they clasp their children to their chests or perch them high on their shoulders. She slips off her thongs and joins them, the slimy mud beneath her feet oozing against her ankles as her body yields and sways with the flow of the incoming tide. Within an hour the water in the lagoon will be over their heads and they will have to swim for it. Around her neck is a plastic bag with her back-up CDs that she had fastened to her wool sweater before she ran from the house. The sweater is itchy and sticky hot; she would like to remove it, but how? In the brief exposure to radiant heat as she ran to the fire-truck, the plastic bag had melted and the discs are welded now to her sweater, all one messy accretion. Plastic? How stupid of her. Why didn't she grab one of the calico shopping bags that hang on the coat rack beside the back door? Hang? Or should that be hung? (For what could be left of that coat rack?) Luke is beside her, grasping her arm now and holding her to him as if at any moment the tide might drag her away. 'Are you alright?' he keeps saying. 'Are you alright?'

'Of course I'm alright,' she says, crossly, for it is anger rather than fear that is going to carry her through this night.

By now it is dark. The sea is lit with an eerie orange light and the moon glows red over the water. Behind them are the burnt-out sandhills. In front of them they can see nothing but smoke, can hear only the muffled boom of the fire as it roars along the headland.

How long before the noise of the blaze begins to recede? Before police vans arrive at the other side of the lagoon and a man emerges from the smoky gloom and squawks at them through a megaphone? Rubber duckies are inflated and they are paddled across the narrowest stretch of water. Luke and Anna continue to look about for the Watts, and for Gil, but there is no sign. They stumble out of the rubber ducky and onto the opposite shore and there, in a dripping huddle, they learn that they are to be driven to a church hall ten kilometres down the road where they will be given dry clothes and spend the night. There is no possibility of returning to their houses, or what's left of them, since the area has been declared a possible crime scene. In the morning it will be cordoned off and the police will move in to look for signs of arson. Arson? They saw the fireball fall out of the sky with their own eyes.

Inside the dusty church hall, blue camping mattresses are laid out across the floor in neat rows. Bedraggled-looking strangers mill around the side walls or slump onto the mattresses. An old woman limps past Anna, held at the elbow by a young fireman. Her hair has been singed to within an inch of her scalp and her eyebrows are burnt away. 'I can't blink,' she says. 'It hurts too much.'

Anna sits on the nearest empty mattress while Luke fetches them sandwiches and drinks from the kitchen at the rear of the hall. Here relief workers are distributing supper. She swallows the water he brings and sips at the black luke-warm tea, bitter with tannin. Luke takes only a single, half-hearted bite from his sandwich before easing himself down onto his elbows on the mattress. Suddenly the adrenalin has washed out of him; he pats his wife on the knee, rolls over onto his side away from her and within seconds is asleep. How typical, she thinks fondly, gazing down at his soot-streaked face; this man could sleep anywhere.

But she, of course, is wide awake, and can only lie on her back and stare up at the vaulted roof. Some kind of faded banner hangs from the central beam, something about a sesquicentenary of white settlement. On the far wall, high above the door, is a wooden notice-board inscribed with the numerals *1914–1918*, and below this are the names of the dead, black-etched in the polished wood. She closes her eyes and begins to doze, waking with a spasm of pain in her shoulder. Somewhere in the hall a baby is crying and she turns onto her side, adjusting her arms to relieve the cramp. As she does so she brushes against a pillow of soft flesh, a child, and instinctively she knows who it is. *At last*, she sighs, for it's the boy. Here he is, dressed only in his underpants and snuggled up beside her. And oh, she could weep with the relief of it. For weeks she hasn't seen him and now, suddenly, he is here. And she no longer has any desire to sleep, to blot out the hideous night, but only to lie here and gaze on his angelic form. From time to time his open mouth sighs a warm breath and his eyelids flutter in deep sleep as all the while his humid body lies nestled in against her ribs. With her finger she traces the rise of his high forehead, brushing aside the unruly whorls of fair hair that cling damply to his skin. How fine his bones, how graceful the curve of his limbs. Ah, she says, so you have come back to us. I knew it, she murmurs. I knew you were indestructible.

Dawn brings an eerie, smouldering calm.

When they stumble out of the church hall into the smoky morning light, they are surrounded by the charcoaled remains of a holocaust. Across the lagoon, the southern end of the beach is a crust of glowing embers. Behind Rittler's Point, sheets of corrugated iron are strewn on a carpet of ash. The trees are black skeletons with crowns of scorched foliage, a rust colour that is like a pale imprint of the flames.

'You people are bloody lucky,' says a young constable, striding up from the road with a cheery air of self-importance. 'It's a bloody miracle. Rittler's Point is gone, burnt out, but the fire went right through Garra Nalla and only three houses lost. Only three.' He is shaking his head. 'You people must have done your homework, that's all I can say.'

Yes, but which three, they ask? And he describes the position of two shacks, both uninhabited, and the home of a family on the edge of the reserve where the fireball hit.

But still they don't believe it until they see it; see their house standing more or less as they left it, rising up, bald and charmless from the blackened remains of their garden, the greenhouse of shade-cloth melted, the bushy tomato trees lying in shrivelled fronds.

They open the back door and it's as if they are on a film set; everything is coated in a thin layer of ash. Near the door is a dead bird, singed along both wings; it must have plummeted down the chimney and flapped its way across the floor. Luke is startled. With an expression of horror he kneels to examine the carcass, lifting the beak and turning the head toward him. 'Oh no,' he sighs, 'that's the bird. That's the one I told you about, the bird in the banksia tree.'

'Are you *sure*?' Anna stares at the stiff form on the mat. He must be mistaken. It can't be that bird. This is just a common wattlebird, one of the predators of the garden, no loss to anyone.

'Yes, that's it! That's the bird. Wouldn't I know it?'

She looks at him in exasperation, amazed to see that he is distraught. Untying the knotted handkerchief from around his neck he begins gently to wrap the bird in its folds and all she can do is turn away. Now she is angry again; with everything that has happened he is crazily upset about this ... this one bird! She leaves him kneeling in the hallway and heads for the bedroom; all she can think of is how filthy she is, how much she longs to shower and change her clothes. Once she is clean again, everything will be alright; then she can begin to think clearly. But when she gets to the door of the bedroom she stops, and puts a hand to her mouth. There, on their bed, is the navy-blue sweater that Luke had discarded before running out into the yard. At the centre of its bunched folds is an ugly black hole where the wool had caught alight and burnt through to the thick cotton coverlet below. When she lifts the sweater, the coverlet is seared with a brown scorch mark. Somehow an ember must have made it into the house and blown onto the bed. But how? Where? She looks up at the small panes of glass high in the old sash windows and sees for the first time that the middle pane is open. It must have exploded outwards, leaving a clean hole, so neat she had not at first noticed it. The ember had blown in and landed on the bed, on

Luke's sweater. The wool had smouldered, and smouldered, but had not blazed, and the ember had burnt itself out. Anna stares at it, at the sweater that almost caught alight but didn't, at the house around her that might have burned down and is still standing. It would be a relief to cry, but her eyes remain dry. Right now she doesn't have it in her; she is too tired, and she is too dirty. She will cry later, she tells herself, and begins to unbutton her borrowed shirt. But then she hears Luke calling out to her. 'Annie! Annie, come here!' She finds him out on the front veranda, staring down to Gil's house, which is now visible below them because the trees have been reduced to denuded sticks. And there is Gil, out in the yard, raking the charred embers from around his water tanks. 'Thank God!' exclaims Anna, and they jump from the veranda and break into a jog. As they approach the black spikes of what were once Gil's gateposts, Luke shouts, and Gil looks up and waves. Such a casual wave, as if they had just been away for a trip to town.

'Have you seen the Watts?'

'They were on the rocks with me,' he says. 'They got evacuated to Brockwood. They're probably back by now,' he nods in the direction of the bluff. He takes out a neatly folded handkerchief and wipes the sweat from his eyes. 'No-one dead,' he says, 'so there you are.'

The settlement of Garra Nalla has survived a perfect firestorm. A sudden descent of dry air had combined with gale-force winds so precipitously that the fire-trucks were left stranded in the hills, unable to make it to the coast in time. Unknown to them, as they stood at the shallow end of the lagoon, the people of Garra Nalla were surrounded on three sides by burning bush; within a ten-kilometre radius of the settlement the winds were blowing in four directions at once and the roads were impassable. The Watts had been driven onto the rocks below, and later, over a lukewarm beer in his kitchen, Alan describes the terror of clinging to those rocks, the disorienting sensation of radiant heat coming at him from one direction while the cold wash of ocean surf broke across his feet. He feared then that his children might slip from his grasp and be swept away, and at that moment his dread of the water had been greater than his fear of the fire. And there is a quaver in his voice now as he glances across at Zack, who is absorbed in playing with his Gameboy on the couch.

'Hostages to fortune,' says Gil, who has wandered up to join them. 'It's all different when your kids are with you.'

That evening, without a word to Anna, Luke slips out the back door and wanders alone through the wasteland of the nature reserve beside the highway. Here the fire had been at its fiercest. In other areas some green remains in the canopy, despite the swathes of blackened trunks and pale russet foliage, but in the reserve every tree has been torched. Not a blade or leaf has been spared. A series of thin stunted sticks that were once young trees jut up out of the ash like primitive totems. Where the fence had run he can see a line of blackened nails, and where the fence-posts stood, clusters of coach-screws. Further in, where the bigger trees had put up more resistance, broken trunks lie splayed across a carpet of ash, whispering thin drifts of smoke.

In all the wind-funnelled anarchy of burning bush, the tidal wave of flame and smoke, Luke had been fearful, yes, but not unnerved. But looking around him now at the charred ground, the blasted earth, the logs leaking smoke, he is gutted. It's as if not just the land has been singed but his body with it. He stumbles, weeping, through the powdery ash, climbing over the still-warm charcoal of the fallen trunks, and he is back in the delivery room, two years ago, when Anna had given birth to the boy; his tiny, curled-up body with its grey translucent skin, his dark, wine-red lips, the pinkish white of his eyelids, closed to them for all time. This child of their loins, only seven and a half months old, dead in the womb; their dearest boy whose heartbeat had one day stopped, lapsed into silence, with his parents unawares, thinking that all was well, that nature was taking its course and that their lives were going along just fine. In those bleak hours after they had cleaned the sticky blood from Anna's body and wheeled her into a pale blue hospital room, the hospital counsellor asked them if they wanted to give their child a name, and they nodded, blankly, and said yes, it would be a good idea. But in the numbness of their grief, no name presented itself and thereafter they had come to think of him as 'the boy'. It seemed so much more intimate than any given name. And now all this grey ash, bringing it all back to him, that other day, the day he thought he had put out of his mind once and for all, a day on the harbour, just the two of them and the skipper of the hired boat, and the boy's ashes in a tiny ceramic vial, and Anna collapsing onto the deck and he, alone, stepping to the edge of the boat and sprinkling the ashes over the white-tipped waves. It was a cold day, and he had worn the navy ribbed sweater, the one that at the height of the fire he had discarded on the bed, because he could not bear the thought that it might come to any harm, and because it reminded him too much of other damage. But the ember had landed there, and the sweater had burnt anyway, and in its thick smouldering resistance it had most likely saved the house.

Anna sits in the dark of the living room and frets for Luke's return. Where is he? Why has he just gone off like this, on his own? The phone tower is still out and she has walked over to Gil's and Rodney's and up to the Watts' but no-one has seen him.

'He might be a bit shell-shocked,' says Bette, who is standing in the kitchen, scrambling eggs on a camp stove. 'Alan's like a stunned mullet. He just sits on the deck and stares out to sea.' She nods towards the deck where Alan is slumped in a canvas chair. 'What about you, are you okay? Want to stay and have some supper?'

'I'm fine,' says Anna, 'and I should go back. Luke might be there by now.'

She walks home through the blighted hamlet, the ground still warm beneath her feet. Inside the house the phone is ringing, reconnected at last, but it's only her mother. 'I can't find Luke,' she says, hearing the panic in her voice. 'We were up at a friend's place and he just disappeared.'

'Why don't you take the car and look for him?'

'Mum, the car is burnt out. And the garage.'

'Can you borrow a car?'

'I don't think so. Mum, people have got their own problems.' She doesn't want to talk about it now. Her mother sounds annoyingly distant and Anna says, abruptly, that she will ring back.

There is nothing to do but wait, and sweep up the ash.

It's late in the evening when she hears him walk up the drive, and she drops the broom and runs to the hallway. Luke is standing there, just inside the back door, and she sees that he has been crying.

'Is it that bad?' she asks. She has never seen Luke cry, not even once.

He shakes his head. 'Not the fire,' he murmurs. 'Not the fire.'

'The boy?'

He nods, unable to speak, and stands on the spot, as if to take another step is entirely beyond him. She puts her arms around him, steadying herself because he is heavy, and she absorbs the shudder and heave of his body, clasping his back and drawing him into her. And they stand there, in the doorway of their home, and they hold one another for a very long time.

That night the boy comes to Anna in a dream. And this is odd, because she never dreams of him, but tonight here he is, at the back door. The garden is as it was before the fire, perfect in every detail, mellow and bathed in afternoon light, and the boy is in the open doorway, waving. But before she can wave back, the figure in the doorway has dissolved into the light. And she wakes, crying, silent tears that stream down her cheeks and wet the pillow. The tears go on and on, soundlessly, beyond her will, until, after a while, she turns over onto her back and lies there, dry-eyed and staring up into the dark.

*

On the third Sunday in December the people of Garra Nalla gather together on the bluff to celebrate their deliverance.

It's just after five on a balmy evening when they spread their picnic things, their chairs and their tables along the blackened knoll that overlooks the sea. A barbecue is out of the question since there is still a total fire ban, but a feast of dishes is laid out on rough trestle tables that Bette has draped with white cloths. Beside this she has set up a small bush conifer for a Christmas tree and hung it with tinsel and coloured lights. Mercifully there is no wind.

Not everyone in the settlement has come. There are some who are still in shock, unable to go back to work; others, it is said, are too traumatised even to leave the house. But Bette is determined to have a party. 'For the children,' she says. 'They must see that the adults are coping.'

The men are subdued but they do their best and set up an improvised cricket pitch on the old tennis court. After dinner many of the families walk home, but a few remain, the women lounging on the Watts' sundeck. Anna is feeling a little drunk, and light-headed in the heat. She closes her eyes, and leaning back into the warmth of the wall, begins to drift off. Bette nudges her, laughing, and offers to fill her glass. 'Wake up,' she says, but Anna declines with a shake of her head. She smiles woozily, and looks over to where the men are clustered, like a flock of birds, at the edge of Alan's unlit barbecue stand, their elbows resting on the warm brick. She sees how intimately they lean in toward one another, as if to catch what is being said, and this is something she loves, this intimacy when men are together, away from women; in sight but out of reach. And she is thinking that she might go off the pill soon, that she is ready to try again. Life is so unpredictable: one cannot postpone decisions forever in the belief that things will be better down the track. What if, one day, there is no track? … and she begins to doze, drifting back into the warm slipstream of her reverie. Out on the horizon she can see a lone sloop, tacking across a stiff breeze. Its red sails are swollen in the wind, and the way they tilt against the sky is mesmerisingly lovely. Then she sees a figure on the lagoon, sitting upright in a small skiff and paddling out to sea. And the shape of this slight figure is familiar. She jerks her head upright, squinting into the sun, for it's hard to see clearly and the glare off the water is blinding. And yes, it *is* him, it's the boy, and she sees now that the sloop is for him, is waiting to carry him to his next destination. Ah, she says, so you are leaving us. So you are on your way at last. But it's okay, it's alright; yes, she thinks, I am ready for this, and she raises her arm in a soft salute. Thank you, she says. Thank you for staying with us all this time.

'Look!' says Bette, pointing across to the lagoon, and the women on the deck look over to where a dozen or more black swans have come out from the rushes to feed on the water. 'We haven't seen them since the fire. Oh, look, that will cheer Alan up. Their nesting grounds around the lagoon were burnt out and we wondered if they were dead, or flown away for good.'

'Alan!' She is on her feet at the edge of the deck and calling out to the men beside the barbecue stand. 'Look!' she says, 'the swans are back.'

The men look up. Luke turns, and waves to Anna on the veranda, who waves back.

When they return home it is all that Luke can do to undress and fall into bed. He has accounted for more than two bottles of red and there was beer to begin with and later some hits of Rodney's tequila. All the way down the road from the bluff he had floated in a haze, blind to the stricken trees and the burnt ground. And now he is in deep sleep, lost in a dream of birds; the swallows from under the eaves are making one of their wild raids on the garden, swooping and diving at dusk; the glossy black cockatoos screech from their perch in the she-oaks; a pair of sooty black oystercatchers glide along the tide line, their black wings and red beaks profiled against the white sand, while out to sea a flock of gulls feeds on the rippled surface of the ocean. And somewhere in there, lost to view, is the phantom of the bird on the banksia bough, and he sighs and groans in his sleep, for he'll never see that bird again, and he still doesn't know its name.

In the bathroom, Anna is taking her time, brushing her teeth in a slow rhythmic motion, her mind a blank. She wipes her mouth and stares at her face in the mirror, brushing her hair back with soft, hesitant strokes. Then she puts down the brush, picks up her pill packet and drops it into the white plastic bin beside the sink. From the bedroom comes the sound of Luke, his light snore travelling down the hallway. But Anna is wide awake, and hungry. She closes the door of the bedroom and goes into the kitchen to make toast, after which she will trawl through the cable news networks and wait for sleep to ambush her. The blinds are still up and she eats her toast beside the window, looking out to the red light of Mars, low over the horizon in the north-east. Miraculously, not all of the she-oaks in the garden burned. There is still a cluster of them in the south-east corner and she listens to the sound of the wind whistling through their canopy, that eerie siren song, and she remembers how it felt to sit in the canoe with the boy nestled against her chest while Luke paddled them across the lagoon; the long slow glide of the boat across the black water.

Turning, she takes her tea and returns to lie on the couch with her feet up, and thumbs the remote control so that the ghostly images of the television come instantly to life in the dark.

Author's Note
Readers of Henry Lawson will recognize references in this work to his poem 'The Fire at Ross's Farm' and the short story 'Bushfire'.

AMANDA LOHREY was born in Tasmania, where she lives today. Her first novel was *The Morality of Gentlemen*, published in 1984. It was followed by *The Reading Group* and then *Camille's Bread*, winner of the Australian Literature Society's Gold Medal and a Victorian Premier's Literary Award in 1996. Her most recent novel is *The Philosopher's Doll* (2004). She is also the author of two *Quarterly Essays*, 'Groundswell' and 'Voting for Jesus'.

LORRAINE BIGGS was born in Western Australia, where she worked on pearling boats, in the field with geologists and in aerial reconnaissance before completing three years of fine art studies. She moved to Tasmania to take up post-graduate studies in 1992. Her main focus is painting, and her work has been widely exhibited. In recent years, she has also worked collaboratively with composers, architects and writers.